# The Va

# Crusades: Book 1

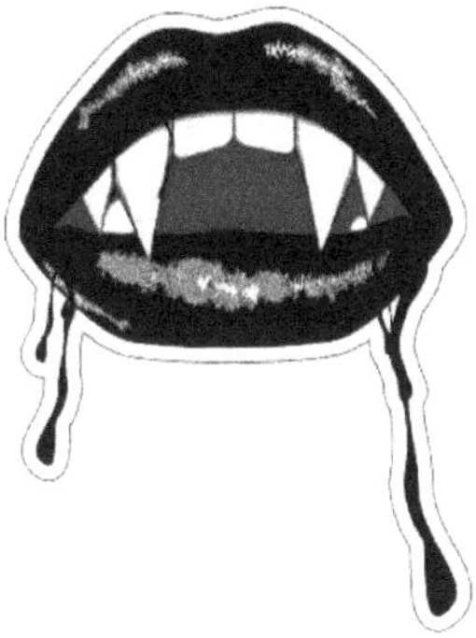

# The Acquisition

J.S. Roach

The Vampire Crusades: Book 1

The Acquisition





e-book ISBN-13: 979-8-9899942-6-7
Paperback ISBN-13: 979-8-9899942-4-3
Hardback ISBN 13: 979-8-9899942-5-0

Cover design by: Susan Roddey
Edited by: Lynn Picknett
Layout by: Jason Roach
Printed in the United States of America

# *Dedications*

To all the fans out there who have purchased my books. To everyone who has believed in me over the last two years and to my writing community who inspires me daily. Last but not least, to my husband who has been my rock during the writing process.

# *Acknowledgments*

Special thanks to Susan and Lynn for all the hard work they've both put into making this a reality. I love you both dearly. A huge thanks to everyone who has shown up at events and supported me and my company. We look forward to seeing you all in the future.

# Prologue

The thumping club music could be heard from the outside parking lot as the man dressed in a black Armani suit exited his car, striding slowly towards the entranceway. His shaved muscular bare chest was visible from behind his unbuttoned jacket. The building looked like an abandoned warehouse of some sort. The flashing strobe and laser lights could be seen through the windows surrounding the upper parts of the warehouse.

"I.D. please!" The man on the door said.

The mysterious guy pulled his wallet from the back pocket of his form-fitting pants and handed over his I.D.

"That'll be fifty," the doorman said, reaching out his hand.

"Man, the price of clubs has gone up over the years," he said, digging through his wallet for a fifty-dollar bill.

"This is the best show in town. We can't keep putting it on for free," the doorman snipped back.

"Ah, yes. And no one should expect you to," the guy commented. "Forgive me, but I'm from out of state. Where exactly are we again?"

The doorman stared at the strange man wondering how he didn't know where he was. He casually said, "Charlotte."

"Where?" he yelled, struggling to hear over the bass-thumping.

"Charlotte. Charlotte, North Carolina," the doorman shouted over the overwhelming music. Now he was deaf too? What was with this man? Lost and deaf? The poor bastard.

"Ah, yes. Thanks," he replied and walked into the club, leaving one very confused doorman staring at him.

The dark, smoky venue was vast with many smaller rooms off to the sides. The dance floor was in the center and multiple bars lined the walls. He gracefully walked up to one of the bars and ordered a shot of whiskey. It wouldn't have any effect on him, but at least he would blend in. He panned the room for his next conquest. There were so many attractive men out tonight. Which one did he want? His good looks and charm would ensure he'd get anyone he wanted. No problem there. The hard part was choosing. Suddenly, in walked the most gorgeous one of them all. A young man - probably mid-twenties - came strolling up to the bar with a group of friends. His strong features - were mostly hidden behind his thick, dark brown locks, which tumbled attractively to his shoulders. His white shirt, half unbuttoned, showed the light, mocha-colored skin stretched across a chiseled chest and the start of a six-pack below. The front hems of his shirt hung down snugly enough to outline the bulge in his dark jeans.

"Whatever he's having, put it on my tab," the mystery man said, pointing towards the piece of fresh meat who'd entered the bar.

The bartender handed the new guy his drink, pointing towards the man who'd paid for it. The two locked dark brown eyes for a brief moment as the younger one raised the drink up in a "Cheers!" Then he disappeared off into the abyss with his friends, but it wasn't long before the mystery man spotted him on the dance floor.

Grabbing another drink from the bar, the man casually walked onto the dance floor. Sliding up behind the young guy, he pressed his body up against him while reaching around him and handing him the drink. The guy seemed receptive but continued dancing. It wasn't long before arms were wrapped around shoulders and lips were making contact.

Pulling apart, the young man said, "Hey! I'm Vic! What's your name?"

"Ezra. Wanna go somewhere...you know... more... intimate," the mystery man replied thickly.

"Sure! Whatcha got in mind?" Vic answered, smiling intensely, while pulling open Ezra's jacket to run his hand down his chiseled body.

"Follow me," Ezra said softly into Vic's ear, taking him by the hand and leading him off into a dark hallway and out the door marked "Exit Only."

"Where are we going?" Vic asked. "I gotta tell my fri..."

"It's ok. We won't be out here long," Ezra interrupted, then pushed him up against the door that closed behind them.

The kissing started slowly, growing heavier till they were sliding tongues down one another's throats. Losing all sense of control, Ezra gave one swift pull on Vic's white shirt, and the remaining buttons cascaded to the ground. Ezra moved his lips and tongue down Vic's now sweaty body, briefly stopping at his neck to inhale his sweet aroma, then moving down to his nipples, sucking and swirling his tongue around each one.

Ezra could tell Vic was in heaven. Arrogantly he assumed this was the best sexual experience anyone had ever given him. Ezra reached his hand down to the bulge in Vic's pants. It was now hard as a rock and straining to escape. Vic lowered the Armani jacket and Ezra felt the sudden pain of fingernails running down his back. It sent chills down his spine, and he let out a moan of pleasure. He lowered himself to his knees and used his teeth to unbutton Vic's skin-tight jeans and lowered the zipper. He wasn't wearing any underwear and it turned Ezra on even more, yanking the pants down and spinning him around to face the door - exposing Vic's perfect bubbled ass for his taking.

Ezra slowly rose from his knees and pressed his body closer to Vic's, holding his hands above his head. He slowly began kissing the back of his neck, moving around to the side. One hard smack to Vic's ass and he felt the adrenaline pulsing in his jugular vein as his lips moved around to the side of his neck.

It was at this moment of immense pleasure when Ezra lost all control, sinking his sharp fangs into Vic's throbbing neck. The crimson velvet flowing into his mouth and down his throat was the most satisfying taste he'd ever had. Poor Vic though. He knew what he was going through. He couldn't speak. His vision was fading, and he wouldn't be able to fight for fear of Ezra ripping out his throat.

Yes, Ezra had once been in his shoes some four hundred years ago. Now, the light around him would continue to fade, and before it was all over, his naked body would be lying on the ground - Ezra on top of him - draining everything but the very last drop of blood.

# Chapter One

## Some Years Later...

Victor sat on the edge of a pier thinking back to that night. The night his life had changed forever. No. Literally, forever. There were times when he wished Ezra would have taken every last drop of his blood instead of letting him turn into this beast he'd now become. Now, seemingly all he could do was prey on others to survive. He couldn't stay in any one place for very long. The local police would start to catch on to the random disappearances and bodies turning up with fang marks on their necks. On this day he found himself on the outer coastal banks of North Carolina. It was off-season so the tourist traffic had died down and it was quite peaceful. The sound of the ocean beating against the dock, the howling of the wind as a storm drew closer. It all seemed to give him a sense of tranquility – however briefly.

It'd been years since he'd seen Ezra. What was he up to? Where was he? The thoughts passed through his mind unbidden as he looked out over the ocean. The last time they were together, there had been a huge argument. Over something silly, really. Ezra wasn't amused when he came home one night to his - once abandoned, now notorious - fully decorated house for Christmas. Flashing lights were in every nook and cranny. However, that wasn't what sent him over the edge. It was finding Vic, or Victor as he now preferred to be called, standing in the living room pouring vials of glitter all over himself. A whole rainbow of iridescent colors sticking to his muscle-sharp wet body.

"Hey! Look! I'm sparkling! And no sunlight required!" He delighted, as Ezra walked into the room.

"God damnit! How many times do I have to tell you? Vampires do not fucking *sparkle*!" Ezra shouted. "Now clean up this mess and take this shit down before someone finds out we are here!" He turned on his heel, walked out the door, and disappeared into the night again.

To this day Victor still got a laugh out of the incident, but that was the last time he'd seen Ezra. He never returned to the place they referred to as home. Can you give a vampire a heart attack? You can supposedly kill them with a stake through the heart, so why not? If his theory was true, Victor figured the shock of coming home to noticeable flashing lights and the mess of glitter all over the floor had probably caused his heart to give out.

With the absence of Ezra, Victor now spent his days now fending for himself. He'd turned into the one thing he'd vowed not to become - a killing machine. He made sure to drain the life out of every victim he claimed. For one, he didn't want the hassle of having to adopt someone and show them the ropes of vampirism. It was easier to end it once and for all.

Having arrived in the outer banks only a few days ago meant he had plenty of time to figure out who would be his latest victim. The ocean was a vast dumping ground for the remains. It would be a while before anyone would associate the bite marks with a possible vampire. They very well could've come from some undiscovered sea creature. It's possible. Wasn't there some film back in the 1970s where sharks terrorized a beach town? His memory seemed to fail him after all these years. He continued to survey the landscape while sitting on the dock, guesstimating the distance across the sound. If the body was weighed down, it could take weeks before it would even be discovered. Hell, it may never even make it to the surface.

This was the life he now lived. Carefully planning every move since there was no longer anyone around to do it for him. He didn't mind it, though. Even when he was among the living, people got on his nerves. He no longer thought of them as human. They were simply there as prey.

To hell with their pettiness over the smallest of things - like Ezra and his lack of appreciation for holiday decorating and a damn good joke. Anyways, he couldn't sit around all day and contemplate life's biggest challenges. It was time to find a place to live.

One of the best things about being a vampire was the money. Over the years, one tends to gather quite a bit of it when the government thinks you're dead. Currencies change, and it gets easier to manage. These days everything was digital. There were no longer dollar bills to carry around or deposit into banks. Come to speak of it, banks were pretty much a thing of the past too. Everything was now accessed through a cloud-based two-authentication system that controlled all of one's finances. It made his life easier. One less thing to worry about.

It didn't take him long to figure out which piece of property he wanted to acquire. Walking back up the pier, he looked up, seeing a large house high on the hill. It was perfect! It overlooked everything and would provide easy access to the dock for when he needed to drop the prey. The large open windows gave off something of a creepy vibe as if the house was watching something or someone. He immediately fell in love with it and was thrilled to discover it had recently been listed for sale. How convenient! It seemed everything with this move was falling into place. It was officially time for him to start over.

# Chapter Two

## Several Months Later...

The house had been easily acquired thanks to his cloud-based finances. And spring had set in, with tourists starting to flood the islands. It would be non-stop for the next several months, but Victor didn't mind. The more people around, the less likely it would be noticed that someone was missing. To blend in, he'd gotten a night job as a bartender at one of the local gay bars - the Cruisy Surf was the name of it. He hated the name, but it provided extra income to replace what he had spent on the house, which happened to be working out as he had planned. Once or twice a week he'd bring some poor miscreant home from the bar, have a little fun with them, and just before letting them have the best orgasm of their life, finish them off by piercing his fangs into their necks. No one had even noticed there was a corpse count of at least eighteen floating somewhere down the Currituck Sound, probably turning up miles and miles away down the coastline, though he'd heard nothing on the news.

Tonight's shift at The Cruisy Surf was different. For what was supposed to be a busy weekend, there sure weren't very many patrons walking through the doors. It was a Friday night and Victor figured as it wore on, more would come. A few hours later a young man in a ball cap, Blondie t-shirt, and jeans walked up and took a seat at the bar.

"What'll ya have?" Victor asked, wiping the counter in front of him. He'd probably wiped the same spot twenty times already.

"A whiskey sour," the patron replied, holding his head down and seeming to hide behind the peak of the hat.

"Sure, but I'll need to see some I.D. please," Victor said, wanting to make sure the guy was legal to serve. After all the progress in currency management, verifying age was not something they'd mastered yet.

"Here ya go," the man tossed his driver's license onto the counter.

"Thanks, Charlie!" Victor said, reading the guy's name off the license while calculating his age. And with his charming Latin smile, Victor continued, handing the I.D. back to him. "One whiskey sour coming right up. Oh, and the name's Victor. Let me know if you need anything."

"Thanks," Charlie responded.

"I've never seen you around here. Is this your first time? Where are you from? Are you traveling for vacation?" Victor quizzed, trying to make small talk. He hated doing it, but in this industry, it was something you absolutely had to get used to. It came with the territory.

"Yes, this is my first time here. I'm from Roanoke Island, and no - I'm not on vacation. I live about forty minutes from here, and this is one of the only places outside of town I found to visit," answered Charlie, still holding his head down slightly.

Victor slowly reached over, tucking his ring and middle fingers under Charlie's chin, and lightly lifted it up. A brave move in this day and time. He noticed Charlie jump back a little then hesitantly give way and lift his head.

"Wow!" Victor exclaimed. "Excuse me for saying so, but you're gorgeous."

"Thanks." Charlie blushed.

"Why are you hiding all this gorgeousness behind the hat," Victor asked.

"I'm not really out to many people. Kinda don't want to be recognized," Charlie replied as he lifted his hat to reposition it onto his neatly trimmed black locks.

"Ah, I see," Victor empathized. "I was once in those shoes. It's a hard path to walk. Hey, man, if you ever need someone to talk to, I'm always here."

"Thanks, I appreciate that. Can I get another?" Charlie sucked down the rest of his cocktail.

The night went on and business remained slow. The two of them continued to chit-chat back and forth between the ever-so-occasional customers who would come up to the bar. The more Charlie drank the more forthcoming with information he became, typical for anyone under the influence. Victor used this to his advantage. It was all part of the hunt. The more he learned about the catch, the easier it was to gauge how much it would be missed. He learned Charlie was a college student working towards a master's in social sciences and wanted to work with LGBTQIA youth. He was about to turn twenty-five. Not much older than Victor, well, in people's years. Living people, that is. Victor also learned how Charlie had recently gotten out of a horrible relationship that ended mainly because he'd chosen not to come out to his family.

"So, if you don't mind me asking, how do you plan to work with LGBTQIA youth, and not tell your parents you're gay?" Victor cautiously asked.

"I haven't figured that one out yet," Charlie sighed. "Someday I'll tell them. It wasn't the right time… Now is not the right time."

Victor later went on to find out why it wasn't the right time. The parents were footing the bill for his studies, and Charlie didn't want to run the risk of them disowning him and losing the funding for his education. *Fair enough.* But if the night kept going the way it was heading, he wouldn't have to worry about who was footing the bill. Victor felt confident he would make a good candidate for his next victim.

As the night came to a close, Victor insisted Charlie come back to his place. After all, he was in no condition to drive since Victor continued to insist he "have another."

He followed up with how he didn't want to hear about a drunk driver who'd driven their car off one of the Highway Sixty-four bridges. Victor could be very persuasive, and what Victor wanted, he normally got in the end. In fact, he'd learned from one of the best. Vampire's charm, he called it - like it was some kind of special power he'd inherited.

Taking Charlie's keys, Victor told him to stay seated at the bar while he finished closing up. It was only about another thirty minutes before he was helping Charlie into the passenger seat of his car. Traffic was extremely light at two in the morning, and the drive was quiet. He wondered if Charlie had passed out. Hopefully not. That would take the fun out of everything he'd planned.

As they pulled into the drive, Charlie's head shot up.

"Duuuuude! Thissshh's your house?" he managed to mumble.

"Yeah, isn't it great! Wonderful view of the ocean. Wait till you get inside." Victor drove the car into the garage underneath the house.

Victor watched as Charlie staggered up the stairs to the first level.

"Woooowwwww!" he exclaimed, taking in all of the openness and enormous windows looking down onto the water. He pulled himself together, trying to sound sober saying: "Yeeeaaahhhh, bartending is not this lucrative. What else do you do?"

"Well," Victor started to reply. He'd gotten this question many times in the last couple of months and had prepared a fool-proof answer. "It's our family's beach house. I've been living here while I... um..." his mind went blank. *Well, there goes that.* He'd forgotten the lie he'd told so many times before.

"Oh, okay," Charlie said, not missing a beat.

He'd made it. Charlie hadn't even noticed he'd screwed it up. But why had he screwed it up? He felt something was adrift. He couldn't put his finger on it at the moment.

# Chapter Three

## The First Time...

Victor watched as Charlie roamed about the house, checking out each of the six bedrooms, three full bathrooms, and the octagon-shaped office looking out over the sound. The lights outlining the pier below were the only illumination visible at this time of night. He commented constantly on how lavish it all was - well beyond his means as a college student. Victor let him enjoy the moment. After all, it was going to be his last.

Finishing the grand tour, Victor took Charlie by the hand and led him back down one of the staircases to the living room on the main level. Taking a seat, Charlie continued to ramble randomly about past relationships, college courses, and parental disagreements. Victor watched him closely. Somewhere along the way he'd lost his hat and the dark hair on the top of his head was a bit ruffled. His long oval face had the most adorable cheekbones that were flushed pink. Gorgeous hazel eyes sat above them, naturally giving off a seductive vibe which sucked Victor right in. These features were something he'd never even considered with the other prey. Maybe he was off his game tonight. As Charlie babbled, Victor slowly placed his hand on his knee - and the talking came to a sudden stop.

"I'm sorry. I didn't mean to startle you," Victor said, slowly starting to lift his hand. Charlie apparently had other plans. He placed his hand on top of Victor's and pressed it back in place.

"You didn't. It's... been a while since someone has touched me," Charlie revealed.

"Oh," Victor said. "How long has it been - if you don't mind me asking?" Though he couldn't figure out why he cared in the first place. *Come on! Get it over with.*

"Probably, a year. Maybe longer," Charlie answered.

"Well..." Victor said, looking up into remarkably seductive eyes. He slowly started to lean in, aware of Charlie doing the same. It wasn't long before their rosy lips touched briefly and they pulled back, looking deep into each other's eyes. Victor could tell they both were longing for it.

He rushed back in, cupping one of his hands gently

around Charlie's face - locking onto Charlie's youthfully soft lips. Briefly opening his mouth to breathe, Charlie slipped his tongue inside, wrestling it around. Victor closed his mouth around Charlie's tongue, sucking in while moving the hand from his face down to the slightly muscular peck. He gave it a light squeeze and continued down to the hemline of Charlie's shirt.

Charlie raised his arms as Victor quickly hoisted the shirt over Charlie's head. His eyes moved up and down Charlie's torso, taking in the beauty of the college boy's naturally athletic build. Realizing Charlie was returning the favor, Victor raised his arms and let his loose-fitting T-shirt glide over his neck. He watched Charlie toss it across the room, then dove back down for more.

Victor's lips pressed against Charlie's alluringly soft ones, slowly moving down his body, stopping slightly below the jawline - nibbling and licking at the neck. The jugular vein pulsing with adrenaline. He opened wide to bite down but stopped shy of doing so and continued down his body.

The nipples were the next stop on his journey. Pierced nipples at that. He swirled his tongue around each piercing, slightly pulling on each one with his teeth.

"Oooooohhhhh," Charlie leaned his head back, letting out a pleasurable moan. Victor could tell he was doing something right, but again, why did he even care? It was going to be over soon. But for some reason, for once he didn't want it to be.

He left the nipples and slowly worked his way down the happy trail of fur leading to the waistline of Charlie's pants. Charlie reached down, unbuttoned, and unzipped them. Victor took this as an open invitation to continue. He gave a slight pull to the waist, and Charlie lifted off the couch, giving way for the pants and underwear to smoothly slide down, and off each muscular, hairy leg. Victor tossed them somewhere across the room. Who cared where.

Victor stood up and began lowering his jeans and boxers while admiring the view lying sprawled out on the couch before him. It startled him when Charlie jumped up before he could lower himself to hover over him.

"What's wrong?" Victor asked, watching Charlie's naked body stride down the hall and into one of the bedrooms. He followed behind him.

"I figured this was your room," Victor heard Charlie say as he entered the room.

"It is…" He replied, as he wrapped his arms around Charlie and lowered him onto the king-size bed.

Victor could sense the passion filling the room as they rolled back and forth across the bed - one on top of the other. He noticed the glistening sweat beads building up on Charlie's chest and one of them slowly falling onto his. It was the most pleasure he'd had since that night some years ago.

"Aaaahhhh," he let out a gasping breath as the two became one. His eyes closed and rolled into the back of his head in pleasure. He'd lost all sense of control, which was something he'd normally not allow himself to do when feeding, but something about this was different. There was a strong connection between the two of them. He could feel it, and not in reference to the particular one joining them at the hip. Trying to shake it, he reached up and pulled Charlie closer to him, matching his rhythm with every thrust. The vein in Charlie's neck pulsed beside him. He could hear it in his ear - throb, throb, throb - with each pulsating heartbeat. Turning his head towards the vein, he began to aggressively kiss Charlie's neck - sucking, nibbling, massaging.

"Oooooohhhhh…" he heard Charlie let out quick deep breaths and felt his body collapse on top of him. Victor rolled him over, climbing on top of him. And with that, he closed his eyes and lowered his body, nestling his face into Charlie's neckline.

# Chapter Four

## The Morning After...

*Someone actually gave him the time of day. Someone who showed they care. Someone who'd just made the most passionate sex... no wait... love to him, and he wasn't ready to let these moments go.* These were the thoughts running through Charlie's head as the warm morning sun beamed down through the double skylight. He cracked his eyes open to see Victor lying beside him, still fast asleep. He smiled.

He told himself he was doing it again - getting attached way too early. It happened every time. It wouldn't be long before he'd planned his whole life around getting away from his parents and moving into the large ass house. If he moved away, he wouldn't have to come out to them. He could be himself and no one would have to know. He didn't understand the big deal with coming out anyway.

Yes, it's good to be honest with yourself. That he'd already done. But in today's age, it seemed more in vogue to tell the world you were a flaming homosexual. Even if you weren't flaming. Just shove it in people's faces. Why don't you? This was how he felt.

This was how his mind worked, leaping jerkily from one thought to another. He was surprised he'd been able to go to sleep at all, even after his strenuous workout with Victor. Normally, he relied on nightly doses of melatonin and the occasional Ambien to get to sleep. He'd at least get a good five restful hours. But last night was the best sleep he'd had in a very long time. Probably another reason he was in such a great mood.

He decided to get up, stop by the restroom to relieve his burning bladder, and head to the kitchen. Coffee was definitely a necessity. He stumbled out of the room quietly, trying not to disturb his ever-so-charming host. Once in the kitchen, he looked around for the coffee maker. There wasn't one. How could you not have a coffee maker? This was a prime piece of real estate in every household. Oh, well. He opened the fridge to see if there was anything to snack on. He didn't care. He was utterly making himself at home. But when he looked inside, it was empty. Not even a single condiment. Now this was getting strange. No coffee *and* no food?

"Good morning."

A deep voice startled him into a jump, and he slammed the fridge door by accident. "Hi. I'm... sorry. I was hungry and... where did you come from?"

"It's ok. I haven't been to the grocery store yet. We can pick something up on the way to get your car," he heard Victor say before turning around, only to wind up nose-to-nose with him.

Locking eyes, Charlie leaned in for a kiss, even though the weirdness of there being no food in the house hadn't worn off.

"I'm so hungry I could eat you," he joked before planting a kiss on Victor and slapping his bare ass. "Go get dressed. I'm sure you don't mind if I shower. Not like there's a shortage of bathrooms in this house. Now… where did my clothes end up?"

Charlie's naked ass scrambled around the living room searching for the articles of clothing that'd gotten tossed all over the room the night before. He clenched them to his chest and ran off to the closest bathroom. Peering out from behind the door, he saw Victor remaining in the kitchen with the biggest smile. He blew a kiss toward him and closed the door.

Despite acting like a giddy schoolgirl, there was something still bothering him. If this was the family beach house and Victor had - he assumed - been staying here long enough to have a stable job, why hadn't he been to the store? Why did it even bother him? Other than the fact of him being hungry, it really wasn't any of his concern. His rampant mind joggled question after question while the hot water ran down his body. He reached for the soap only to discover there were no bathroom toiletries either. "Guess there was no time to shop for that either," he mumbled out loud. Thankfully, the washcloth hanging on the wall would allow him to scrub off the previous night's activities, and the hand towel lying on the sink was barely enough to pat himself dry.

Despite the obstacles, the shower was still refreshing enough. At least he wouldn't go home smelling like the town whore. Emerging from the bathroom in his tight burgundy boxer briefs and tapping the dampness from his bare chest, he looked around for Victor, but there was no sign of him. Curiosity got the best of him, and he started to rummage through his bedroom. He walked into the office area but got distracted. The windows looking out over the sound from the pentagon-shaped room made the house appear as if it were sitting directly in the water. But as he looked down, he saw Victor walking back towards the house from the dock below. What was he doing down there? Maybe he feeds the ducks every morning? Who knows? Perhaps it was none of his business. Who was he kidding? It *was* none of his business.

Before Victor could get back up the hill and inside, he quickly grabbed the towel in one of the other bathrooms to finish drying off. He pulled his shirt over his head and shook his hands through his shoulder-length hair to spread out the wet curls. He loved how his hair naturally curled when it was wet. But before he could remove his hands,

Victor snuck up behind him and slid his arms around his waist.

"Jesus! Dude! Where did you come from? I thought you were…" Charlie stopped before he let on he was snooping around the house.

"Down at the docks," Victor interrupted. "I saw you looking down from the office windows. I figured you were almost ready to head back to your car."

"Is this the part where you tell me you're not really taking me back to my car, and in reality you're some serial killer who's going to chop me up into little pieces and toss me into the ocean to float away at sea?" Charlie joked but had started to freak himself out so much, he almost believed it.

"Well, maybe not into little pieces…" he heard Victor say, feeling him kiss the back of his neck. Squirming to get away - partly from being ticklish and the other part from fear - he made a mad dash for the front door.

"Come on, you silly goose. Let's get you some breakfast," Victor said, chuckling. Charlie felt his hand on the small of his back but hadn't heard him come up behind him.

*Why are the creepy ones always so cute?* His mind wandered as Victor continued to usher him out the door and down the stairs to the car - Which was no longer parked in the garage.

"When did you move the car?" Charlie asked.

"This morning, before I came back inside," Victor answered.

*Lies! There was no way he could have done that. I would have heard the garage door open.* Charlie got in the passenger seat. *Should I even be getting in this car? I have to…I have to get back to mine.* This mental argument continued the entire fifteen-minute ride until the car came to a stop. The rundown building started to put his mind at ease when he realized it was actually a restaurant. He also realized he was only a hop and skip from his car should he need to run.

Charlie was charmed by how Victor held the door for him as he entered the restaurant. He even carried his tray for him to the remaining available table in the dining room. The place was hopping that's for sure. The uneven floor made it wobbly and a pain in the ass to sit and eat, but at least there was food.

"Hey, I'm sorry if I've appeared a little distant this morning," he said as he dug his fork into the grease-reddened hashbrown omelet. "I can be a bit of a monster if I don't get food when I need it."

"A little? You called me a serial killer. I'm not sure I can be your friend anymore." Victor grinned.

"Yeah, I did. I'm sorry. I guess I kinda freaked myself out with you not having the bare necessities of life anywhere in the house…And I don't normally hook up with people, especially on the first night. Can't say a date, because it wasn't a date…and… I'm rambling again. Aren't I? Hey, are you not going to eat? You're missing out." Charlie shoveled another spoonful of hashbrowns into his mouth.

"It's all good. I'm not really hungry. I woke up and had a late-night snack," Victor replied, slowly raising his head enough so his eyes glistened with seduction and lips formed the perfect grin.

Charlie immediately melted into his eyes, but it wasn't long before reality kicked back in. "Wait a minute! If there was no food in the house, what did you eat?"

"I went out. You know, hit a drive-through, and came back to chow down," Victor replied.

Again, something wasn't adding up, but the heart attack, that was the half-finished omelet on the plate before him, took precedence over his Nancy Drew half-assed conspiracy theories. He decided to let it ride. After all, he was probably never going to see this guy again. The good ones always disappeared.

Charlie finished devouring the breakfast he learned Victor had paid for while he'd excused himself to the restroom. *Awe, how sweet of him.* It wasn't long before they were back in the car and heading the two blocks over to the bar where his car awaited.

"It was great! Thanks for last night, the shower, breakfast…" Charlie babbled with a laundry list of thanks before he noticed Victor holding up his hands to interrupt.

"It was my pleasure. Will I see you again?" Victor asked.

"I don't know. Maybe?" Charlie said, opening his car door and crawling in. "It was great and all." He waved and started to drive off. Looking in the rearview mirror, he saw Victor walk back into the bar. His heart dropped. He immediately missed him, but his conspiracy theories had freaked him out enough he felt he'd probably made the biggest fool of himself. He was sure there were plausible explanations for everything that'd put him in this state. Who knows? The guy probably didn't even really want to see him again.

# Chapter Five

## A Week Later...

The following weekend rolled around, and Victor found himself busier than ever. The check-out line was backed up with prey, and he could feel his thirst rising from within. Actually, his thirst had drastically increased since his little encounter with Charlie. Every time he thought about him - about that night, about his tight ass, and those pulsating veins - his thirst heightened. His once-a-week kill had turned into a nightly routine ravished with prey, which boiled down to not being able to get him off his mind. He wondered if he'd show up at the bar tonight. Poor kid was a little freaked out but surely, he'd come around.

He hadn't been to a grocer in probably twenty-something years, yet here he was with no clue what the popular commodities were these days. It wasn't like they sold blood-flavored chips or Reece's Blood Cups. The only thing possibly good enough to have suited his taste was the raw meat, but even then, that was pushing it. He ended up following the other customers around, adding whatever items they added to their carts to his. It was the most hodge-podge cart ever. But one thing's for sure, there would now be an immensely overstocked kitchen with cabinets bursting at the seams of the prey's everyday snacks.

It was odd to him how he even cared. He'd never gone out of his way to make one of them happy or more at ease with their surroundings. Normally, he had his fun, drained their life, and dumped them in the sound. It was obvious this one was going to be different. He could see himself saving him, keeping him around, turning him.

He'd vowed though - to himself and on his mama's grave - he'd never turn anyone without their consent. Killing them was one thing, but to curse them with an eternal life was way worse. He thought about all the sheep who believed eternal life came from some kind of religious experience and scoffed. He'd watched all his friends mourn his loss, move on, get married, have children, grow old, and be buried. It was eternal hell. And though he'd come to terms with it, he couldn't bear the sight of watching someone else go through it. Be heartless. Kill 'em and get it over with. That's what had always gotten him through. Now here he was loading the car with groceries after a one-night stand.

The drive back wasn't too long, but with the long waits to checkout, he was running behind. It was a Memorial weekend, and The Cruisy Surf was opening early. He lined the countertops with grocery bags and covered the dining table with the additional toiletries most guests would expect. There wasn't enough time to put it all away and redecorate the entire house, so he put the perishables away and jumped back in the car.

When he arrived at The Cruisy Surf, people were already queued at the door waiting to get in. Damn, these homos didn't waste any time. He still had to measure the alcohol and prep the bar before any of them could be served. Fighting his way through the herds of people gathered around the front door, he managed to make it inside fairly unscathed. Maybe a hair or two out of place, but he'd be fine. The same hair that had constantly given him issues over the last … well too many years to count. For him, it had to be perfected every day. Not a hair out of place, though it never would cooperate.

Surprisingly, it hadn't taken him as long as he'd expected to organize everything together and have the bar in tip-top shape. And just in time too. The herd had turned into a mob and was now pushing themselves through the doors.

"Oh, girl, you know he's got the bootie cooties.

Don't mess!" he heard one of them say as they sashayed past the bar and into the restroom. Bootie cooties… what the hell did that even mean? Oh, the prey was going to be lit tonight.

"Excuse me! Bartender! Can I get a drink over here?" Another one yelled from the far end of the bar.

"One second. Be right there," Victor answered, making his way over to the guy at the end. But on his way, something caught his attention - a conversation taking place across the room. Another joyous perk of being a vampire - sonic hearing. He homed in on the group while trying to listen to the poor sap place his drink order.

Table:

"I couldn't believe it. Here in our own…"

Bar:

"Bud Light, please with a…"

Table:

"The news said it could have been an accident but…"

Bar:

"Hey, while you're getting his, how 'bout a rum and…"

Table:

"They're going to do an autops… puncture wounds…"

Bar:

"Hey! Excuse me! Are you listening?"

"I'm sorry. I spaced out there for a moment. What can I get you?" It was too much. There were way too many distractions to focus on one tiny group on the other side of the room. He'd have to check the news later to see what it was they were talking about. For now, though, there were dozens of sheep at the trough, and it was his job to water them all.

The night continued as crazy as it started, except now most everyone was an ungodly amount of sheets to the wind and half naked. Navy men on leave now paraded around shirtless with their tight muscular chests and eight-pack abs – even dead you couldn't get those abs. The twinks were dancing in their stringed skivvies with their legs wrapped around some pole. The bears were strapped up in their leather harnesses and assless leather chaps. The pups were leashed up and following their masters. Foam flooded the dance floor, looking like a nor'easter had blown in off the coast.

Victor looked around, searching for his helpless victim of the night. Maybe the junkie over there in the corner doing a line of coke off the table. Or how about the guy standing against the wall all by himself? Watching people with their blank stares. No one would miss a creeper. Or what about the guy over there? The one that'd just entered the room. The one walking over towards the bar. The one who looked like Charlie.

Victor watched as the guy climbed up on one of the available bar stools. With the way the crowd was, it would be a while before he could even make it to the other side of the bar. They really should have hired some extra help for the weekend.

He worked feverishly to get the sheep watered as quickly as he could, but by the time he'd made it to the other end, the guy was gone, and a dozen twinks had replaced him demanding their sex on the beaches, tequila sunrises and shots of Red Bull and Jager. Bitterness had started to set in, and he was half tempted to take the whole group to the bathroom and have a Christmas feast, but that wouldn't turn out so well. Still, the ungrateful, privileged, late teens, entitled bastards needed to learn their spot in the food chain. Well, maybe someday. He had to bring himself back down to earth and remind himself how he was once in those shoes many years ago.

Another hour or so had passed and he still hadn't located Charlie or the guy who looked like him. Had he left the bar without a drink? He wasn't out there dancing in the foam, come to think of it, that shit was a huge liability for

The Cruisy Surf. If some slipped and busted their ass out there, they could sue the hell out of this place. But oh well… wasn't his problem. Returning to his search, he panned the room one more time.

He'd all but determined the cokehead in the corner was going to be dinner by the time the bar had closed. He was still propped up on one arm at the table and no one had even noticed he was still inside. He gave the bar one last wipe down, but unexpectedly, he heard the front door close.

"I'm sorry! We're closing up for the night," he yelled from behind the bar. Ready to hide there if they were about to get robbed.

"Yeah, I know," he heard the familiar voice say as they entered the room.

"Charlie? Is that you? What are you doing here?" Victor quizzed as he nervously picked up his ragged cloth and started wiping down the bar again for the fifth time.

"I came in earlier, but the crowd was too much and…" Charlie was cut off.

"Hey, you! It's time to go. We're closing up shop." It was the bar owner's voice as he came charging out of the office.

"Hey man, it's ok. He's with me. But you might

wanna grab the guy over there in the corner," Victor mentioned, pointing over in the direction. "I'm not even sure if he's conscious."

They watched as the owner attempted to carry the guy out the door, glanced back at one another, and chuckled. Victor watched as Charlie walked up and rested his arms on the bar.

"So… any plans tonight?" Charlie asked.

"Hmmmm, yep. I believe I do have plans tonight," Victor replied with a seductive smile.

"Good! Let's get going. It's almost 4:00 AM," Charlie said, turning to walk back out. Victor followed him out the door but realized he wasn't heading toward the cars. Charlie was heading towards the back of the building. Behind the building sex was always fun, but he gave up on the idea when he watched him go out onto the beach.

"Care for a walk?" Charlie posed.

"I think that sounds like a wonderful idea," he replied, catching up to him. "You may have to carry me, though. I've been working all night."

Charlie let out a chuckle and started to stroll down the coast. The sound of the waves crashing against the shoreline echoed in the background. The moonlight shining down, the slight breeze keeping their bodies cool, their eyes slowly adjusting to the darkness. The mood was set, and it was probably one of the most romantic nights of Victor's very long life, except for one thing. The thirst had returned.

# Chapter Six

## An Intricate Allure...

Victor swallowed hard, trying to suppress the urge to drain the life out of this gorgeous creature walking beside him. The deep breaths he took sounded more like he was preparing for Lamaze-style childbirth.

"You ok?" Charlie asked, slowing his pace and placing his hand on Victor's shoulder.

"Yeah, I'm ok. Why?" he said, regaining his composure.

"You sounded like you were hyperventilating a bit. Thought maybe we were walking too fast," Charlie joked.

"Nah, I'm fine. Sorry 'bout that. Not sure what was happening," he lied. "So anyways, you came back for more. You know… you did kinda freak out on me a bit."

"Yeah, well… I had a really great time. Actually, it was one of the greatest times I've had. I figured if you were going to cut me into tiny pieces, I was at least gonna be sliced and diced happily." He paused and gave a devilish grin.

It didn't take Victor long to throw out another tease. "Now who's the one running out of breath?"

He looked up and saw one of the many lighthouses in the distance. Slapping Charlie on the ass he challenged, "Come on. I'll race ya!" and took off in a sprint.

Panting heavily with adrenaline rushing through his dead veins, he turned to check on Charlie.

"Dude…how…*gasp*…can…you…*gasp*…run…so fast?" he barely managed to get out before resting against the wall of the lighthouse and slowly sliding to the ground.

Victor hadn't thought one of his little secret superpowers would show up in a running contest, but it must have. Hopefully, he could come up with something to throw him off. He figured it out quickly when he quipped back, "Nah, I don't run fast. You're just slow."

"Oh, I'm slow, huh? Ha! I don't think I'm…

well… ok yeah, maybe I am," Charlie admitted defeat.

With a win in place, Victor took a seat next to Charlie and placed his arm tightly around his shoulder, pulling him closer. "It's ok… I'm giving you a hard time."

"Not actually, I mean, you could be if you wanted to, but I don't consider a few quips a hard time," Charlie teased.

"Ah, now it's obvious why you came back. You really just wanted my cock? Ha," he taunted, grabbing a handful of his crotch, and playfully shaking it around. "It's ok. If that's what you want, you can definitely have it." They both laughed.

Victor knew there wasn't anything he wouldn't give this boy, but still for the life of him - or lack thereof - he couldn't figure out why. He leaned in and kissed his forehead, his lips lingering. He started to pull back teasing Charlie to reach up and pull him closer, this time locking both of their lips together. The occasional slide of the tongue from one to the other turned into a make-out session for the gods above to see. Detaching his wet rosy lips, Victor locked eyes with Charlie and smiled. With arms wrapped around the other, they squeezed tightly, pulling each other in.

As the sun rose over the ocean, the sandy beaches became clearer to see and the dark cover of night drifted away. All of a sudden Victor grabbed Charlie's hand, pulled him up, and guided him inside the abandoned lighthouse.

The door slammed behind them simultaneously with Charlie being pressed against the wall. Victor pinned his hands and arms above his head, and slowly worked his head between an arm and Charlie's head, pressing his puffy lips against his neck – *thump thump thump thump* – he could feel the adrenaline rushing through his jugular as he sucked lightly. It was all he could do to keep the fangs back as they paasionately desired to sink into flesh. He worked his way up his neck to the base of his ear, nibbling the bottom of his lobe. When Charlie let out a sound of immense pleasure, he knew he was doing something right.

It wasn't long before he released his arms and lifted him in the air while still managing to engage every pleasure point from the ear to the base of the neck. He felt his legs wrap tightly around his waist. His erection fighting to get out of those tight pants and into Charlie's now perfectly aligned, tight familiar hole.

With his hands firmly gripped on each cheek of Charlie's ass, he used his core strength to bounce him up onto a boarded-up window ledge. He lifted his shirt over his head and tossed it onto the dusty floor, pushing him back against the plywood window to admire the view. There they were again. Those perfectly shaped nipples - each with a barbell piercing in them. And he knew exactly where that happy trail was going to lead him.

Victor used one arm to wrap around him, balancing and pulling him closer. He landed his mouth directly onto the right nipple, and swirled his tongue around briefly, moving over to the left, giving it the same treatment. The release of suction and Charlie's gasp of gratification sounded through the open room - echoing up the rounded metal staircase leading to the top of the lighthouse. Victor thought for a moment he'd prematurely released himself from the way his body shook in pleasure. Whatever had happened, he could tell by the look on Charlie's face, he was thoroughly enjoying the attention.

He lifted off his shirt and felt two hands run over his torso. When they reached the top of his waist, he felt a bit of a struggle subsequently at the release of his pants falling to the floor. He looked down and watched as Charlie's hands released the pulsating rod from the restraining dark blue Calvin Klein briefs. It was dripping with excitement. He watched Charlie slide off the ledge and down to his knees. Moments later he felt his hot mouth locked around the veiny shaft. It was everything he knew it would be and more. The delight arising from a mixture of suction, tongue swirling, and a tight twisting hand wrapped around his hard cock sent him over the edge. Victor grabbed the back of his head and thrust forward and as far down his throat as he could. There was the sound of rapture as he groaned with each pump of release down Charlie's throat. *And he took it like a champ*. He rubbed the back of his head as Charlie was cleaning up every drop.

"Damn, man. I'm sorry. It was entirely too good. I couldn't hold it any longer."

"It was pretty tasty too if I might add," Charlie threw out there while wiping the evidence off his jawline.

"Hey, hey! Come here. We still have to finish you," Victor said, kneeling down to eye level. He looked up with anticipation as Charlie rose from the floor, but as he reached up to undo his pants, they both heard a commotion outside.

Cracking the door open slightly, and peering through, Victor noticed something he wasn't expecting and definitely wasn't ready to deal with. He quickly but quietly closed the door and turned to Charlie.

"Come on. Get dressed. We've got to go," he said in a whispering hurry, scurrying around the room trying to find where his clothes had gotten to.

"Why? What's going on? What's wrong?" Charlie quizzed.

"No time for questions right now. We have to figure out how to get out of here without being seen," Victor said while struggling into his pants back on.

"Without being seen? Why? Who's out there?"

Charlie asked, reaching for the door, but Victor grabbed him before he could reach the handle.

"Listen, I'm sorry to freak you out like this..." Victor said trying to pull Charlie's focus towards him.

"Oh, no worries. It's becoming a common thing with you," Charlie interrupted, becoming a bit frantic.

"Please, take a deep breath and listen. I'm not sure how we didn't hear all this, but there's a whole news crew, police, police tape, and a crowd of people gathered down by the water," he tried to explain. "We have to try to get out of here without them spotting us in the process."

"Ooookaaayyyy, but what does that have to do with us?" Charlie asked. "Let's go find out what's going on."

"Two queers coming out of an abandoned lighthouse... It will look conspicuous," Victor thought back to the conversation he'd overheard at the bar. "Not to mention dead bodies washing up on shore."

"DEAD BODIES!!! Who said there were dead bodies out there? We were just... I can't... please tell me... God Damnit!!" Charlie went into a tailspin.

"Nobody said that...shit! I'm sorry," Victor said, trying to find a way to undo the madness he'd created. It might have been better for them to sneak out without him saying anything, but he freaked out. "Look, I overheard some people at the bar talking about a body washing up on shore. I immediately assumed this was the same thing…"

"Oh my God!" Charlie looked at him, "Did you really drop someone's body into the ocean, and now you're freaking out because they found it?"

*Smaacccckkk!*

Silence filled the room and Victor stood in shock at what'd happened.

"I'm so sorry. I don't… you didn't…" he grabbed Charlie, pulled him close, and wrapped his arms around him.

"I did kinda deserve that." Charlie's muffled voice came from the crevice of his arm. "I'm sorry I accused you of doing something so preposterous. It's just…"

"I know. I totally understand. I freaked out and therefore you freaked out. I don't hit people, I don't support people who hit people, and I've never done anything of the like before. I'm so, so sorry," Victor pleaded.

"It's okay," Charlie said while letting the sting fade from his face, tracking down his shirt, and sliding it over his flushed cheek. "Anyways, how are we getting out of here?"

"Well, let's see if we can sneak out. Maybe slip around to the other side and make a run for it. I think we can make it if we move quietly." Victor wasn't concerned about his movements drawing attention, though. Call it another one of his superpowers, but Charlie on the other hand was a mere human, prey for that matter. In his opinion, they were designed to make noise.

He reached for his hand, but Charlie backed away a little before interlocking their fingers. Victor gave him the "really, I already apologized for every aspect of my life" look and together, they exited the lighthouse the same way they had entered - except there was a lot less passion.

The door didn't make a sound as Victor slowly pulled it open. With barely enough space for them to slip through, he stepped out, holding the door for Charlie. When it closed, they quietly stepped around the sides of the building until there was no longer a chance, they would be visible to the crowd. Victor tried to listen in to see if he could get a feel for what was going on.

"I can't believe it. Do you see…?"

"There's not much left of it…"

"The cops said it washed up this morning. I hope…"

"The fish sure got a hold of this one. What do ya think…?"

There was way too much noise from the crowd to figure out what was actually being said. They kept cutting each other off, but he could get a good sense from the pieces he was picking up on. All of a sudden, the words he heard sent shivers down his spine, and it confirmed all he needed to know.

"Look at those two holes in the neck…"

His recklessness had gotten the best of him and was now on the verge of exposing him. He looked at Charlie and could feel the sadness welling up inside. Decisions were going to have to be made, and at this point, they may no longer include him.

"Come on," he pointed up the hill, "let's go." And they ran up the dune and out of sight of the spectacle below them.

# Chapter Seven

## The Unexpected Guest…

Emerging over the hill, they dodged their way through multiple empty news vans and pedestrian vehicles in the parking lot until they reached the main road.

"We should get back to our cars. I think we'll be fine to walk along the highway. I don't believe we were spotted," Victor advised. "It's not far from here."

"Yeah…" he heard Charlie say as he tagged along behind him, nearly out of breath.

Victor was sure he'd blown it this time. What a mess he'd created! Time passed in silence as they walked back to the bar. What was it – fifteen, maybe twenty minutes? He couldn't tell. The morning sun was now beating down on his face. Thankfully vampires didn't sweat. The occasional deep breath released from behind, and the quickly beating heart working overtime to pump blood and oxygen, told him Charlie was struggling to catch his breath. He turned his head ever so slightly, enough to see the man who'd shaken his entire existence pushing himself to keep up. Victor stopped and waited for him to catch up.

They walked in silence until they reached the parking lot of the bar.

"I'm so sorry your evening was ruined. Please let me make it up to you. I'd love to take you to breakfast. I'm sure you're hungry, and we all know what happens when you don't eat. Eh?" Victor tried to get him to laugh by making a joke but could tell it didn't go over well.

"I'm actually…*gasp*… not hungry. I think…*exhale*… I'll head home… and get some rest," Charlie responded slowly, taking slow deep breaths and stepping towards the two remaining cars on the gravel. "Maybe…*gasp*… I'll watch the news …*exhale*…and see what's going on around here."

"Will I get to see you again?" Victor asked, worry cracking his voice.

"I don't know, man… I think I've about had

enough anxiety and excitement for one lifetime within the last couple of weeks." His breathing had slowed to an almost normal pace. "We'll see. I'll give it some thought."

"I promise I'm sorry for what happened. Every bit of it, well, except for the cuddling, fondling, and…" Victor found himself nearly begging on his knees for forgiveness. Something he'd never done in the past nor ever pictured himself doing for anyone or anything, especially the prey. But in this moment, right now, he felt like there wasn't anything in the world he wouldn't do to spend eternity with this guy.

"Look, I know you're sorry. I may even forgive you, but I'm going to need some time to get myself together. Figure out what the hell happened today and find some stability. I can't keep having freakouts every time I'm around you," Charlie explained. "I need to figure out if those freakouts are valid or am I freaking for no reason at all?"

"Fair enough, and there may be valid reasons," Victor said, opening the car door for him. "I hope, though, I'll get to see you soon."

"Wait, what do you mean there may be valid reasons?" he turned, looking Victor in the eye, quickly stopped himself from going further. "No. Never mind. I don't wanna know right now. I'm outa here."

Charlie got in the car, closing the door behind him. Victor watched him wave a brief two-fingered peace sign and pulled out of the parking area onto the main road back towards Roanoke Island. He got in his own car and headed back towards the house. Immediately, he remembered there were mounds of groceries scattered all over the house he'd need to deal with before assessing the situation. Rest wasn't really something his body needed, but he would like to at least relax a little before his next shift.

He stopped narrowly shy of the driveway to check the mailbox before continuing into the open garage. It was at this moment he sensed a dark presence he hadn't felt in years. Shivers ran down his spine. Someone was here… in the house. He exited the car, slowly entering the house through the stairway from the garage, not knowing what to expect when he emerged into the dining room. All of the remaining groceries and toiletries were missing, and he heard a voice telepathically ringing in his head.

"We need to talk, Victor."

He looked around the open space of the house but there was no presence to be seen. He yelled out into the emptiness, "I don't have time for games and parlor tricks! Where are you and what did you do with my stuff? That was two weeks' worth of pay damnit!"

The intruder walked through the living room door from the front porch which looked over the brown, murky

Atlantic. He appeared the same as he did all those many years ago in the Charlotte nightclub scene. The suit had changed of course, but the familiar scent of Davidoff's Cool Water cologne radiated the room. It made Victor think of a line from *Titanic* where old Rose had smelled the same damn paint for eighty-four years. He held a chuckle inside while trying to keep a serious face. *Some things never change.*

"Well, hello to you too," Ezra's voice came as he walked a circle around him, looking him up and down.

"Hello to you *too*? You walk in here after so many years and expect things to be jovial? Remember you're the one who left me, and now I'm stuck here to fend for myself because of the monster you turned me into. So, get to it. What is it you want? I've got other things to deal with and stop looking at my ass and tell me where you put my shit." Victor continued to rant. "And for that matter, who do you think you are walking back in here…?"

"Calm down. Your stuff is where it belongs. You never were one to put things where they go, but I'm not here to argue with you about petty prey items. Though that ass is looking much tastier than the pile of shit you called stuff." Victor rolled his eyes and tried to walk away. "I'm here because you've created quite a mess of things. I'd suggest you pack up and get the hell out of this Godforsaken little town before a pack of vampire hunters come knocking down this gorgeously stained 1980s pine door. Such a shame to let that happen to such an antique."

Victor stood in shock at what he'd heard. What the actual fuck was taking place? Had Ezra returned to parent him after all these years? Because this wasn't going to fly. And an antique? 1980s? Really? Anything from the 1980s should never be considered an antique. Classic maybe, but never antique. No, not at all. None of this was okay.

He dropped his belongings on the table which once held the mound of toiletries and groceries and finally escaped into the kitchen, where he placed two glasses on the counter, filling them halfway with his newly obtained bottle of Jack Daniel's. It wasn't how he'd initially planned to be using it, but there was no way he was going to make it through this little charade without some type of alcohol.

"I'm handling it," Victor stated, "Here! Have a drink."

"Thanks. But I'm curious. How might you be handling it?" Ezra continued his parenting. "By playing house with one of the prey?"

"Ah! There it is. That's why you're here." He took a big gulp of his drink. "You're freaking jealous I've found myself interested in someone other than you. Do I need to remind you, yet again, you are the one who left years ago with no explanation?"

"I'm not concerned with whom you love. I *am*

worried about how you're going about it, how you're toying with the prey instead of making the turn, and the Thanksgiving feast you've created in the sea which continues to wash up on shore. And if it makes any difference, I never left. I've always been close by."

"Close by? What the fuck? Now you're some kind of undead creeper, watching over my every move? You trip me out, you five-hundred-year-old piece of shit!" Victor poured himself another drink ignoring Ezra's almost empty glass.

"Not creeping. It's my duty to watch over my children, and to make sure they do not expose our kind. Like it will be yours if or when you decide to turn this boy," Ezra said, finishing off his drink. "You need to know what you are getting into. What you have already gotten into. And I assume you do plan to turn him at some point, otherwise he'd be washing up on shore."

"I know what I'm getting into. I've had all of eternity to think about it, and…" He was cut off.

"You have no clue what an eternity is. You've been around not even a hundred years. So you've made it through the eighties and nineties. Disease can't hurt you when you're already dead, but it sure ate your friends from the inside out. Oh, yeah, and the horrible, death-ridden pandemic in the early 2000s, when your lungs no longer bring life to your body, there's nothing left for a virus to cling onto, but it sure wiped out the rest of your family. Would you have made it through those things had I not turned you?"

Here it was. The same argument about how gracious he should be because Ezra couldn't control his fangs. Goddamnit! He was tired of having this conversation. The anger had built up so much he couldn't control it, and before he knew it, the once-filled glass went flying across the room at Ezra's head. As if in slow motion, he watched him dodge to the left and the glass flew past him, hitting the banister and showering fragments of glass on the floor.

"That's real cute, you know. Throwing a temper tantrum because you don't like what you're hearing. All you Gen Xers are the same," Ezra stated while looking at the shattered glass, then back over at Victor. "Always pitching a fit when someone calls you out on your bullshit. Well, it's time to man up. Take some accountability for your own actions."

"What the hell is that supposed to mean? You know, I've not had this much anger and turmoil in my life since you left, and I don't intend to let it back in," He walked over to the front door, holding it open. "Get your shit and get your ancient, toxic ass out of my life. Exactly like you did the last time, and don't come back! And one day you're going to realize the world is a different place, a more accepting place."

"Lose your fucking delusions, Victor. The world is not ready to know of our real existence. Let them watch their movies, have their fantasies, and continue to dream on. I'll go…for now. Give you some time to cool down," he stated, slowly walking back out the front door. "But I'll be back at some point. Probably when the hunters are burning down your house because you refused to listen. Can't let anything happen to this gorgeous door."

"GET OUT! And don't bother. I don't care if I ever see your rotted face again. Stay out of my life!" Victor slammed the door immediately, but Ezra was gone before it had even closed. As if he'd disappeared - literally.

Exhausted from the events of the morning and feeling a bit tipsy from the double shots of Jack, Victor stumbled into the bedroom and crashed down on the bed, looking up at the skylights as a cloud blocked the sun from beaming in. He let out a sigh, rolling over and turning on the news. It was time to get a grip on reality and see what exactly was going on.

The local news had started a twenty-four-hour coverage of the findings. Two bodies washing up on shore within a day wasn't quite the norm around these parts, probably not anywhere else for that matter. Blurred-out images flashed across the screen as the reporters discussed what they thought might have happened.

"Kaplin, it's hard to say at this moment what could have killed each of these victims. There have been many speculations surrounding the cause. Some say a coincidence, some say a cult with some type of neck branding, and others even suggest vampires are walking among us here in Kitty Hawk, North Carolina. We won't really know anything for sure until the medical examiner has completed the autopsy. What we do know is none of the victims seem to have families or many friends in the area. It seemed they were loners people wouldn't miss."

More videos played across the screen. This time displaying images from the lighthouse this morning. The prerecorded news reporter was standing upwind on the beach using the lighthouse as the perfect backdrop for her unscripted discussion of the morning's event. It wasn't her story that caught his attention, but what was captured in the background. In the distance behind her, there was a perfectly clear image of two people exiting the lighthouse and running around the corner.

"SHIT!!!" He jumped up and started pacing the room. "What the fuck am I supposed to do now?"

It seemed no one had even noticed. The screen returned to news anchor Kaplin and he said, "There is a search out now for the two men seen exiting the lighthouse behind Miss Atwater. We're not sure if there is a connection to the bodies or if they merely didn't want to be seen. However, authorities would like to know more about why they were there and what they saw."

"Shit! Shit! Shit! Shit! Shit!" Panic set in as Victor

jumped off the bed and began pacing the bedroom. What was he going to do now? He needed to get to Charlie. They'd been seen and the police were now looking for them. What if they got to him first and he told them about the strange happenings that continued between them? What if… what if all of this blew up in his face and he'd have to admit how Ezra was right?

# Chapter Eight

## The Outing…

Charlie sat in his living room watching the news. Though exhausted, the events of the morning had him on edge, his mind running, and wide awake trying to determine what he'd encountered. On one hand, there was the wonderful evening he'd had with the most gorgeous man. Someone he thought too pretty to ever find interest in him. On the flip side, there was the abrupt end to said evening. *Why all the secrecy? Why was this guy so mysterious? And the comment at the end… maybe there are reasons? What was that supposed to mean?* The never-ending slew of questions continued to roll through his head like a hamster running on a wheel.

The television played in the background. Tally Atwater was giving the latest update from the scene of this morning's ravaging events, but Charlie had lost himself in his own mind of questioning.

*Doo doot doo doot doo*

The sound of his phone ringing pulled him out of his daze. He answered before even looking to see who it was.

"Hello?"

"Charlie? It's your mama," the voice on the other end of the line said.

"Hi, Mom," he said with a sigh.

"Charlie…why are the police looking for you?" she asked hesitantly.

"What?" he interrupted.

"And who was that boy you were running around with? What were you doing all the way out in Kitty Hawk?" she quizzed. "Aren't you supposed to be in school?"

"Ma, slow down with the questions. What are you talking about?"

He got up from the chair and started pacing. "First off, I don't take summer classes. You already know this.

But what's this about the police looking for me?"

"I saw it on the TV. They caught you on video behind that Batwater woman while she was tellin' us the news. You and that boy. Charlie, who was that boy?

"It's Atwater, Ma."

"What?"

"Atwater! Now what about the police?" He asked, avoiding the question regarding Victor.

"Well, the news said the police were looking for you and that boy. They wanna know why you were hanging around the dead body that showed up on shore," she paused briefly. "Charlie… did you have anything to do with those dead bodies? My Lord, my son's a murderer. Dear Lord Jesus, help us. Son, the Lord's gonna help. I just know it."

Charlie brushed off the religious vomit that continuously spewed from his mother's mouth but was immediately reminded of where he got most of his paranoia. Maybe it was a good time to tell her he was a cock-sucking queer. Might sound better than an ocean-dumping murderer.

"Ma…Ma!" he yelled to interrupt her rambling. "I'm not a murderer."

"What were you doing in the lighthouse, hiding from the cops?"

At his wits' end with the interrogation, he opened his mouth and it all spewed out. "I was getting laid, Ma! I was getting laid."

"Oh, well… I guess if you're into that sorta thing, but you two left the poor girl in there?" she continued. "What kinda men are you? I didn't raise you to treat any woman like that."

"Ma… there was no girl! Just me, and the guy! And I'm not telling you who he is because he's a nobody and none of your business." he snapped. Between the stress of the morning and this integration, he couldn't take it anymore. The cat was already out of the bag so he might as well run with it now. Except there was silence on the other end of the phone. "Ma? You there?"

"I am," she responded.

"Ma. I'm sorry. This was not the way I wanted to tell you. I had it all planned out in my head," he explained. "We'd go to a nice dinner, and I would be able to tell you…"

"Let me stop you right there," she chimed in. "A nice dinner wouldn't have broken this any easier. I've always known you were different… A mother knows. But that doesn't mean I want to talk about it, hear about it, or even see the shit on TV. I wish you'd actually been a murderer. That I could fix. This… well… I simply don't want to hear about it anymore. You get this shit straightened out and make it go away before it comes back to bite you in the ass. Get yourself right with the Lord. And get your ass back in school. You were in less trouble when you were in school. Oh, don't tell your father. He'll kill ya."

*Click.*

The line on the other end went dead. He let the phone drop to the ground as he fell to his knees in tears. Relieved it was out, but scared of what the future would hold for his relationship with his parents, his relationship with Victor - and then there was the police. At least he could tell the next boy who came around he was "out." He guessed family holidays and beach trips weren't going to be happening any time soon. *The good Lord just wouldn't have that.*

Charlie awoke, drool running from his open mouth. The room was in shade and the afternoon sun had almost faded away. It was apparent exhaustion had taken over and he'd cried himself to sleep. He pulled himself off the floor - his body too stiff to be in his mid-twenties. Grabbing himself a glass of water, he sat down at the dining room table and proceeded to flip through his phone. There was nothing but article after article on the events happening in the Kitty Hawk area. It all came rushing back to him as to why he'd passed out on the floor.

He jumped up, and hastily headed towards the shower. He knew what he needed to do, but before he stepped out of the apartment, he had to get the drool off his face and the night-before sex off his body. It didn't take him long to clean up and toss on a hat. He grabbed his keys and was out the door in no time. His destination… the Kitty Hawk Police Department.

He made the forty-minute drive in silence, aside from the occasional role-playing conversations he had with himself along the way. He went over and over what he was going to say when he arrived at the police station. By the time he pulled into the parking area, he was sure he had it perfectly rehearsed.

The building housing the police department was not at all what he expected. It looked like a small house at the center of a residential area - with a car park in place of a grassy yard. It was kind of sketchy, so he cautiously got out of the car and walked inside, peering behind himself to make sure no one was following him.

The entire police department sat behind an acrylic wall. *A bit of an overkill.* He walked up to the counter. *Maybe for protection? Maybe left in place after the Covid times? Who knew?* The name badge of the person sitting at the desk behind this clear monstrosity read Deputy Susan. She appeared to be in her mid to late forties, overly anorexic, and had bleach-blonde hair pulled into a ponytail. Her leathery skin told she'd spent way too much time laying out on the beach. He walked up as she was putting her cigarette out in the over-filled ashtray.

"Excuse me, Ma'am," he said quietly. He wasn't sure whether he should speak as if he was in a library or what the proper etiquette was inside a police station.

"Yes?" Deputy Susan's raspy voice replied, barely looking up from her crossword puzzle.

"I need to speak to an officer," he said. "Is one available?"

"Johnny! Get out here! Someone needs to speak to ya!" she yelled. "They don't pay me enough to help out around here. He'll be with ya shortly. Take a seat over there."

"Okay. Thank you," he turned to find a row of chairs lined against the wall. He took the closest to the door in case he had a quick change of heart and wanted to make a run for it. It took Officer Johnny nearly ten minutes to emerge from his office and open the swinging half-wooden, half-acrylic door into the lobby.

"Ya needed to speak with me?" he asked.

"Umm, yeah… I…"

"Wait a minute," Officer Johnny interrupted. "You're one of them there guys that was on TV aren't ya. I'd recognize ya anywhere the way they are showing it on repeat. Come on back here. Let's have a chat."

Charlie followed Officer Johnny through the door and down the hallway. He appeared harmless, but he was still skeptical. He was probably in his late fifties and looked a bit out of shape. Maybe he hadn't been out in the field for a while, though his skin tone said he'd seen his fair share of sunlight in his days. There was a deep feeling of regret building in Charlie's stomach. Even though he was at a police station, he didn't feel very safe and protected. They didn't seem like the type of people who were very accepting of others who were different, but instead of dashing out the door, he decided to proceed… for now.

He entered Officer Johnny's office, making himself familiar with his surroundings. There were awards plastered all over the wood-paneled walls for the many accomplishments he'd accrued over the years. Pictures of his family lined the bookshelves along with a few knick-knacks here and there. Stacks of documents sat on the corners of the desk.

"Have a seat there, sir," Officer Johnny directed. "Now, I appreciate ya coming in. We were hoping one of ya would. Can you tell me what happened out there?"

"Well, sir, that's just it. I can't tell you what happened out there. My friend and I decided to camp out in the old lighthouse building the night before. When we awoke, there was all this commotion going on outside. It kinda freaked us out, so we tried to sneak out of the building and run away." Charlie rubbed his clammy hands on his pants to dry. After all, it was partially the truth.

"A camp out, huh," Officer Johnny said. "Aren't ya boys a little too old for playing camp?"

"We'd been out fishing and had a few drinks. We were too intoxicated to drive and didn't want to get behind the wheel." This was the best excuse he'd probably ever come up with. "When we realized the lighthouse was open, we camped inside to sleep it off."

"I see," Officer Johnny pulled his steepled hands up to his chin. "And after sleeping it off, as ya say, that's when you heard the noise and decided to sneak out?"

"Yes, sir."

"Hmmm… Ever watch them reruns of Criminal Minds? I saw an episode once where the uh... What do they call 'em? Unsubs? Yeah… that's it… Where the unsub tried to insert themselves into the investigation to throw off the police. They totally walked up in there and told them some kinda bullshit story like this. They say it happens more than ya realize," the officer casually mentioned.

"Sir, are… you implying … that's what I am … trying to do here," Charlie said shakily, getting nervous, thinking he was about to go to jail for trying to do the right thing. Well… right enough to get him off the hook. He looked up from his feet and into Officer Johnny's eyes.

"Nah, I solely thought I'd give ya a little tidbit of information. Scare the shit out of ya a little bit. Watch ya squirm," he replied. "But nah, those people were crazy. Ya seem to have a good head on your shoulders. I believe ya. I'll write ya story down and get ya to sign it so we'll have it on file. Be right back."

Charlie sat, doing exactly what Officer Johnny had wanted - squirming in the chair while he waited for the him to return. His paranoia had him not fully trusting Officer Johnny's request, but when he brought the paperwork back to the office, it matched everything he'd said nearly word for word. He jotted his signature down and was quickly was escorted back to the lobby with an invitation to return should he remember anything else. *What an odd request.* If they believed what he'd told them there would be no reason to return with further information. *Maybe it was out of habit. They probably say it to everyone who comes in and gives a statement. Who knows?*

Before heading home there was one more place he

needed to stop. The Cruisy Surf was only a short fifteen-minute drive from the police station, and with all that had happened in the last twenty-four hours, it would be a shame to not stop by and let Victor know how he'd taken care of the police situation. If, he'd even known about it to begin with. Feeling very pleased with himself, he drove off into the night.

# Chapter Nine

## The Interview...

The Cruisy Surf sat empty on N. Virginia Dare Trail as Victor pulled into the parking lot. He didn't expect it to be too busy tonight since a dead body had washed up not far from the building. People were on edge. He was on edge if the truth was told. It took him most of the afternoon to calm down. At least one good thing about being a vampire - which Ezra failed to mention during his inaugural feasting on his flesh - would be how sleep is overrated.

As he worked to restock the bar, he heard the door open and the sound of footsteps heading toward the bar. He peered up over the counter when he heard a familiar voice mumbling and then shouting across the bar.

"Victor! Police here wanna have a chat with ya," the bar owner yelled from across the open room.

"Sure thing," he replied "What's up, officers? Can I get you a drink?"

"No, thank you. We're here on the job," they said and propped up on the bar. "We wanted to ask you a few questions about last night. I'm sure you know what we're talking about?"

"No, sir. I'm not sure I do," he lied. "But if there's something I can answer, I'll be glad to help."

"Good to know. Good to know," one of the officers repeated. "So, tell us about the lighthouse. We have witnesses who have identified you and another boy exiting it shortly after a body was discovered washing up on shore. What can you tell us about the two of you sneaking out from the inside?"

He felt his own black blood drain from his face as it turned much paler than it already was. He turned around to rinse his washcloth, so his face wasn't visible. His mind running with ways he could get rid of them. *Feast on them, here in plain sight. His boss wouldn't notice.* He would be fast about it and hide the bodies in the walk-in cooler till the end of the night. Wait… Here he was proving how Ezra was right all along. A familiar voice pulled him out of this state.

"Hi officers." The trio heard from behind. Victor turned his head to see Charlie walking up to the bar. "It's me. The other guy in the video. I had a little meeting with one of your colleagues a moment ago and gave him a statement regarding our adventures in the lighthouse last night."

"Well, that's just great except we need to hear it from him as well," the other officer said.

"You mean how we got a little intoxicated and decided to sleep it off in the lighthouse instead of drinking and driving?" Charlie tossed out there while giving a wink to Victor. He'd taken Officer Johnny's little joke and used it to his advantage by inserting himself into the two officers' interrogation.

"Yeah, that's right. We slept it off. Woke up to the commotion and snuck out before we got arrested for trespassing," Victor chimed in. By this time, he could read Charlie's thoughts and their stories started to align. "We were hoping we wouldn't get caught because we'd camped out in an abandoned lighthouse, but it looks like the news caught us at an inopportune time."

"Okay, fellows, we get it. Appreciate your safety and all. If you think of anything else, please stop by the station. We'll be keeping an eye on this bar as we've learned that at least one of the victims was a regular patron here." The two officers tipped their hats and walked out the door.

"You're a lifesaver," Victor said leaning into Charlie hoping for a kiss. However, he stood there perfectly still staring at him. "What? What did I do now?"

"Nothing. Give me the strongest things you've got behind the bar and sit tight. Boy, have I got a story for you," he watched Charlie climb up on the bar stool closest to the wall and begin to unleash the midday events.

"She said all that?" he asked Charlie after hearing the retelling of the phone conversation with his mother. "Are you ok? I know it's hard to deal with. We've all been there at some point and time. Hard to believe, even in this day and age, things are still not as widely accepted as they should be," Victor's mind flashed back to his comments on acceptance from earlier in the day which now sounded hypocritical. "You'd think religious bigotry would have died out over the years, but I guess if it's made it this long, it's not going anywhere anytime soon."

"Fuck religion, and fuck anyone's parent who would rather have their son or daughter be a murderer than a homosexual," Charlie chugged the first drink and Victor was there to immediately refill it as the ever-efficient bartender he was. Besides, there was no one coming out to have a great time at The Cruisy Surf anytime soon.

The two had a night reminiscent of their first one together. Victor was a little more open, though he wasn't as eager, nor did he know how to explain how his five-hundred-year-old boyfriend had returned from the past to act like a parent.

The occasional customer would stagger in from time to time, have a quick drink, afterwards moving on to the next place. At one point a group of military boys came in, sitting at one of the tables near the bar. Victor didn't recognize them as any of the regulars, so he was curious about what they were in town for. He took the opportunity to listen in while Charlie had stepped away to drain his aggressive intake of alcohol.

"It's bad. You know it's bad when they've called us in," one said.

"I heard they want us to close the beaches. Do you know how hard that's going to be?"

"Yeah, they're gonna turn this place into a military town until they get this shit figured out," another chimed in.

"Whoever this sick fuck is, I hope I'm the one who gets to kill 'em."

Victor scoffed as he suddenly remembered the name of the movie he'd thought about so many months ago when he was musing about sharks terrorizing a beach, because in the movie… they also tried to close to beaches. It didn't work then and definitely wouldn't work now. The prey is too entitled and clueless thinking they can stop one of nature's most violent predators. He'd simply have to do better when he disposed of the bodies.

"Whatcha laughing about?" Charlie asked as he climbed back onto his bar stool.

"Those guys over there said they heard the local law enforcement was trying to shut down the beaches. Like that's gonna help them figure out what's going on." He kept chuckling while he poured him another drink.

"Well, it might not be such a bad idea," Charlie said. "If they close the beaches, it will get rid of most tourists. Less people to go through."

"If they do, we're out of a bar and me a job," Victor quipped. "And you, sir, would not be allowed onto the island."

"True. That would definitely suck," Charlie agreed.

"Ah, so you admit it would be a tragedy if you couldn't get on the island to come see me," he teased as he gave the bar another wipe-down from boredom.

"I didn't say all that, but at this point, we might as well just dive in headfirst. I think we've been through enough in this short time to last us a lifetime." Charlie chugged the rest of his drink.

"Oh, really! You're young, baby, and that's cute.

Lifetimes come and go every day." He poured him yet another drink. Anymore, and he was going to beat the record of the first night they'd met, yet he was amazed at how well he was holding it.

"Oh… oh…nah! See… now you're acting like you've had enough of me. You can't…"

Victor quickly cut him off by jumping up over the bar and placing a big ol' sloppy wet kiss on his forehead. "Don't go putting words in my mouth." He slid back off the bar with the biggest smile on his face. "I'll settle down and play house with you any day."

He noticed Charlie about to respond when the few patrons turned their attention to the commotion coming from the front entrance.

"I swear Philipé. If they put me out on that beach one more time, I'm going to scream. This is not what I moved here for. Next time, I'm going to protest on air."

The gasps spread across the room as they watched *the* Tally Atwater enter The Cruisy Surf followed by her cameraman. They dropped their camera, mic, and whatever else on the center of the bar and pulled up a couple of stools.

"Hey, bartender!" Tally screamed. "What's a lady got to do to get a drink around here?"

Victor looked up at Charlie who had all but buried his head inside of his hat, turning to holler back. "What can I get ya?" but the minute he turned full circle, he realized she recognized him.

"How about an exclusive interview for Channel 9 with your very own Tally Atwater?" She flashed her gorgeous smile at him.

"I think that's going to be a no, but I can get you all the liquor you want for a price. What will it be?" He grabbed a glass and flipped it around in his hand.

"Of course, you wouldn't wanna talk. No one wants to talk, and this town stinks! I'll have a margarita on the rocks. Shaken not stirred." She tossed herself back up onto her stool, waved her hand towards the cameraman and said, "Get him whatever ever he wants too!"

"Rum and coke, please," the cameraman said, appearing slightly embarrassed by his coworkers behavior.

"Um, Miss, did you want a martini - shaken not stirred - or a margarita?" Victor tried to clarify.

"A margarita! Duh! They make them for me all the time," she snapped back.

"What a moron," Victor whispered to himself as he quickly made the drinks. "Let's get these drinks made, and get them the hell out of here." He poured a shot of tequila here, and a shot of rum there and slid their drinks across the bar. He made a quick trip down the line to check on the guys at the other end, before turning back to check on Charlie. He found him crunched up against the wall - head buried in his hat - and noticed his glass was almost empty, and this time decided it was best to bring him a cold glass of water.

"Well, hot damn! Both of ya are in here. If I could get one small, little interview. It'd be …"

"Listen, lady! We're not doing interviews. We've already chatted with the police. We're off the hook now, so leave us alone, unless you need another drink," Victor snapped. It was one thing for her to pester him, but to start pestering Charlie - he wasn't going to stand for that.

"Police? Off the hook? Can I quote you?" Ms. Atwater raised her margarita, holding her straw to her lips, she sucked it dry. "Another margarita, please."

He tossed a few mixtures together then slammed the new drink on the counter. "Look, take this drink, finish it, and get the hell out of here. We have nothing to tell you."

"Alright, Alright!" she said, "A girl's just trying to get a promotion and get out of this shit hole. I'm tired of standing on smelly beaches with nasty ocean water. Even standing upwind doesn't get you out of the smell." She pulled the straw out of the new drink and chugged the entire glass, slamming it down. "Come on, Philipé. We're not welcome here. Oh, and don't piss me off or I'll tell the police what you were really doing in there." She winked and swayed the mic from Victor to Charlie back and forth.

Victor followed them out the door to make sure they actually left, before returning to check on Charlie who had nearly passed out against the wall. He took this opportunity to step into the boss' office.

"Hey, boss," he said, "It's close to midnight and aside from the police and the news reporter we've only had around fifteen customers all night. Mind if we close up shop a little early tonight?"

"Not at all," he replied. "Saves me a little on the light bill. Get everyone out. Shut it down."

"Thanks, boss," Victor said, walking out. As he rounded the corner of the bar, he let the army boys know it was time to settle up. Once everything was closed out, cleaned up, and alcohol measured, it was time to go home. Charlie was still passed out against the wall. He walked over to him and gave him a slight nudge.

"Hey, baby… Come on. It's time to leave."

"Wha…I fell 'sleep… in a bar," Charlie tried to stand up from the stool, but almost immediately lost his balance. Victor grabbed him with both arms, lifting him back up. "I don't think I should drive."

"Don't you worry your pretty, little head. Can you walk?" He tossed his arm over his shoulder, almost dragging him along.

"Later, bossman!" Victor yelled as they walked out the door. He loaded Charlie into the passenger side of his car, grabbed a blanket from the back, wrapped him in it, and closed the door. It wasn't too much longer before they were out of the parking lot and heading to the beach house in Duck.

The short drive didn't leave Victor much time to think about the "What ifs?," should Ezra make another appearance at the house - especially now with Charlie in tow. There was no telling where he could be watching from, but hopefully, he would have enough respect to let them have their peace.

The car pulled into the garage - the feeling of being watching lingered over his shoulder, but Victor felt safe for some odd reason. No bullshit would be dealt with tonight. He could feel it in the air. He opened the passenger door and woke Charlie from his drunken slumber.

"Babe, hey, we're home. Can you make it up the stairs?" Victor lightly shook his arm.

"I think I can," He pulled himself up from the car seat, and swiveled his body to get out. Victor tried to steady his flow as he swayed back and forth while going up the stairs. When he reached the top, he stumbled towards the master bedroom collapsing face down on the bed.

Victor rolled him over and raised his torso off the bed to remove the T-shirt hiding his chiseled abs. Furthermore, he undid the button to his pants, lifting his hips and sliding them down his legs. He pulled off and dropped each shoe to the floor before each pant leg eased off. Standing back, he took in the view of the most attractive man he'd ever seen lying in his bed. But before his arousal could take over, he covered him with blankets and turned the lights out. He'd be out through the rest of the night for sure. This also allowed him to take care of some other business.

The thirst was picking up and Victor needed to plant his teeth into someone's jugular something fierce. He headed back to the car, but there was no telling where he was going to end up. No one was on the island at this time of night. Duck was always a ghost town when things weren't open, even if it was peak season. He drove back into Kitty Hawk and found a Walmart out on the main thoroughfare - Croatan Highway. Surely there was bound to be some low life in there no one would miss. He parked the car and entered, wandering the aisles looking for anyone who seemed worthy of being prey. *They all did.* It wasn't long before he found a short nerdy guy with glasses hanging out in the Lego aisle. He slowly approached, stopping shy of where the guy was standing.

"The new Batcave set is amazing! Have you built it yet?" he said, determinedly making small talk.

"Not yet. Can't really afford it. I stick to the smaller sets mostly," the guy replied.

"Listen, man. I… I have it at home if you'd like to come over and help me finish building it." He flashed his charming vampire smile that would normally get him anything he wanted.

"Nah, I think I'm good. With all the murders going on, and whatnot, I'd rather not run off with someone I just met. I don't even know you, dude," the guy said, backing away and gave a slight wave as he left the aisle. "Have a nice evening though."

The guy disappeared from view, leaving Victor standing there in a state of confusion. The smile had always worked in the past. What stopped it from working this time? He was now determined to get this prey. It wasn't long before he found him in another area - this time the video game section.

"Ah, we meet again. Must be fate," he said, flashing the smile again. He could feel the dimple showing.

"Seems like it," the guy said, slowly backing away.

"So which is it? A Playstation or an X-box? You know back in my day they used to have physical discs for each one of these systems. Now it's all streamed online." Victor rambled nervously. He was losing his touch apparently.

"What do you mean back in your day? You mean like sixty-something years ago. You don't look like you're over thirty," the guy said. "I'm leaving now. You're creeping me out. Don't follow me either."

But that's exactly what Victor decided to do. He followed him the rest of the time in the store, then directly out to his car, keeping his distance and out of sight until it was the right time to pounce. The parking lot appeared empty and as the guy was reaching for his door handle, he swooped in, using both hands to grab his head and shoulder, spreading them apart perfectly enough to expose that pulsating vein. He sunk his fangs into his exposed neck and sucked the blood in as hard as he could before letting the guy's limp body fall to the ground. He held on to him by a fist full of t-shirt, letting the blood drip from his face back onto his body. Instantly, he heard a female scream from across the parking lot.

"What the…?" he said aloud. His mind filled with questions. Where did she come from? No one was out here! What the hell does he do now? He dropped the half-alive prey to the ground, letting him continue to bleed out, and started to quickly back away when he slammed right into someone.

"Go! Get out of here. I'll clean it up," he heard Ezra say. "Go!"

Victor fled into the night, leaving his prey, his car, and his dignity behind. What was going to happen? What did he mean by he'd clean it up? Surely, he would be holding this one over his head for all eternity. He'd for sure have to leave town. He'd been spotted. It'd be all over the news. The town would soon find out vampires were roaming the coast of North Carolina.

# Chapter Ten

## The Confession…

His vampiric speed made the roughly two-hour walk back to the beach house seem like he'd flown over everything standing in the way. It's possible he had. He wasn't in a great state of mind. A few minutes and six and a half miles later he found himself looking up at the house from the main road. He hadn't fully wrapped his mind around what'd happened in the Walmart parking lot. *A mistake is what happened. A mistake.*

He entered the house through the side stairs to the game room. Thankfully, he still had his keys with him as he'd closed the garage door when he'd left earlier. He heard the bathroom door open and there stood Charlie down the hallway. They locked eyes.

"What the fuck?" Charlie yelled. "What happened?"

"What do you mean what happened?" Victor suddenly remembered his face and clothes were covered in the prey's blood. He rubbed his hand over his chin then held it out to see a solid brownish-red smear across it. "It's ok. It's not mine."

"What do you mean it's not yours? If it's not yours, then whose is it?" He could see Charlie starting to panic. "Wait, did you leave me here alone? Where have you been?"

"Give me a moment. Take a breath, calm down, and I'll explain everything," he reassured.

"Don't tell me to calm the fuck down. I have put up with enough of this mysterious shit for some time now, making excuses here and there for why you act so differently. Why you don't have food in your house…Why you were hanging out on that dock…Hell, I even went to the police station and lied for your ass. The last thing you are going to tell me to do is calm down!" Charlie shouted as he located his clothes and started to dress. "I want to know the truth, and I want it now! And then, you're going to take me back to my car so I can get the fuck out of here."

"So…, it's not going to be that easy. The car is not

here," Victor replied. "Please…," he held up his hand, "give me a moment to get cleaned up. I promise I'll explain everything."

"You have five minutes! I want some answers!"

He watched Charlie walk off towards the living room, leaving him standing in the hallway with blood still all over his face and clothes. He pulled his shirt over his head and wiped his face before removing the rest of his clothes and getting in the shower. The hot water ran a murky reddish-brown color down his head, over his body, and into the drain as he scrubbed the remaining dried blood from his skin. He let out a deep sigh. Shit really had hit the fan. This was going to be an interesting rest of the morning. He hoped Charlie would be somewhat understanding. Though at this point, he wasn't sure anymore. Shutting the water off, he dried off and wiped away any possible remnants of the prey before exiting the bathroom.

"I'll be there in a moment. Let me get some clothes on!" he yelled to Charlie in the living room.

Silence.

"Charlie, you still out there?" he checked as he pulled up a fresh pair of underwear and all but jumped into his pant legs as he stumbled back out into the hallway and into the living room. That's when he saw the mess lying all over the floor, and the culprit standing in the center of it all.

"What the fuck have you done?" Victor yelled, charging forward directly into Ezra. The two of them hit the ground landing in a pool of blood seeping from the puncture wounds in Charlie's neck. He attacked with every force he could muster, but the tears took over his body, finding himself bent over next to Charlie as Ezra raised himself off the floor.

"I did what I said I was going to do. I cleaned it up," he explained far too calmly. "The poor bastard you started is gone, the woman who saw you is gone, and now the new love of your life is…"

"You bastard! You killed him!" he cried.

"I have not. In the next twenty-four hours, his body will start to turn. You must be present when this happens. He will need blood. Our blood," Ezra explained. "Be sure the blood comes from you and make sure he doesn't drain all of you. He will try. It will take some time before he regains his strength, though I'm hopeful you remember these moments from your own turning. Now, I want you to get your things and get out of here before anyone comes after you. I took the liberty of bringing your car back, but I'd suggest a more discreet form of travel. Maybe you could finally master turning into a mist?"

"I've never been able to change into mist form.

Never had a need to do that. Not sure I can. And what the hell am I supposed to do about all this blood?" He panicked. "What if I forget? What if I don't get him out of here in time? What if he turns without me? What if…"

*Smacccccckkk!* The sting ran down his dead pale face.

"Pull yourself together. We're in this because of you. Now keep your head on straight."

Ezra quickly moved about the house at warp speed cleaning up the mess he'd created, his frustration escalating because of the situation at hand. "I'll get this. Here! Take this and wrap it around his neck. It will help the bleeding and for fucks sake go clean yourself up again. Grab a change of clothes for him too."

Victor wrapped the gauze and bandages he'd been handed around Charlie's neck, also taking the time to raise him off the floor to remove the reddish-brown soiled clothes from his body. He replaced him in a blood-free zone of the dining room then ran to the back of the house to grab some new clothes for them both. Thankfully, they were about the same size.

The anger from the night's events still reverberated within him. Ezra had taken too much into his own hands. Things were happening way before he'd planned. He actually hadn't planned for any of this. He hadn't planned at all. It reminded him of the time back when he was human, and someone took it upon themselves to tell his parents he was gay. Though even that'd gone over better than this.

Once he'd washed and redressed yet again, he brought a towel to wipe down Charlie before dressing him in clean clothes. *I'm not ready to transform into a mist. I can't do it. And I can't ask him to help anymore. It will be even more of a shit show. I'll handle it myself.* His mind was running a mile a minute with what to do next, where to go, and how to get there.

"I can't mist. Give me my keys," he said, laying out his hand for Ezra to place them. He expected another argument on how and why he should be listening to him but with hesitance all he got was a snarky comment.

"Okay, it's your funeral… or burning I should say," he replied, placing the fob in his hand.

"Can you at least have some type of faith in me instead of always cutting me down?" Victor pleaded for some form of acceptance or validation of how he wasn't the total failure he felt Ezra saw him. "I know. I'm stubborn, and I made this mess, but I'm not a complete failure."

Ezra stopped his cleaning and looked him straight in the face. "You're not a failure. You've made some mistakes. Everyone does. We'll get through this. Our kind always does. When was the last time you heard of someone burning a vampire to death? Or jabbing a stake through someone's heart? These things don't happen anymore."

"I haven't really paid attention," he quipped. "But I guess you do have a point. Or maybe they are all in jail instead of being burned alive these days."

"Look, stop panicking or you'll never get out of this," Ezra said, pausing a moment then pointing to the floor. "Now, get him in the car and get out of here,"

"Where should I go?" Victor asked.

"Get off the island. Head down the coastline. If you want, I have a house in Wilmington," Ezra said, picking up a piece of paper and a pen off the kitchen counter and jotting something down. "Here's the address. I'll be there as soon as I can get everything squared away here."

"Thank you," he said, bending down to pick up Charlie.

"Remember, twenty-four hours and he'll need to feed. Make sure it happens."

"Got it. I'll make sure it happens," he said as he carried Charlie's lifeless body down the stairs into the garage, and securely placed him in the passenger seat.

"Shit!" he exclaimed suddenly, running back up the stairs.

"What about his car? It's at The Cruisy Surf," he yelled to Ezra.

"Leave the keys on the counter. I'll take care of…"

"I don't know where the fucking keys are. Probably in his pants which should be somewhere over there covered in blood… I think. I don't know. I…," he ran his hands through his hair. Something he could always remember doing in states of panic.

"Just go! I'll figure it out. Get out of here!" Ezra yelled.

"Okay! Okay!" Taking his cue, Victor got his ass back downstairs, in the car, and away from the life he'd come to know and love.

GPS said the drive would take about four and a half hours from Duck to Wilmington. Pulling out onto North Croatan Highway, he could see the reflection of emergency lights in the sky coming from the Walmart behind him. He pressed on, paying close attention to his speed. Drawing attention to himself was out of the question considering there was a half-dead body in the passenger seat.

A heavy silence filled the car except for the occasional startle of the GPS telling him where to turn.

Crossing over onto Roanoke Island, he thought about the life Charlie had up until this very night. Yeah, he didn't have the best relationship with his parents - or have many friends for that matter - but it didn't mean he deserved to end up like this. Charlie had goals. He was working towards getting an education to bring those goals to life. He wanted to help people. He was one of the good ones. Now it was Victor's job to keep him alive - well unalive - and to explain why the events of the night had taken place. This probably wasn't going to go down very well. Hopefully, he would be understanding, but in all actuality, probably not. He surely wasn't when Ezra decided to strip him from his existence some hundred years ago, and he was a lonely coked-out club kid at the time. Such a shame the events of tonight set things in motion that would change the way Charlie will have to live the rest of his life. Hell, both of them. At least a good amount of lying low was in their future.

The drive to Wilmington went fairly smooth after he got his brain to stop processing a million different scenarios of how he was going to explain the night. The truth. He was going to tell the truth. Whatever happened afterward… well… he'd cross that bridge when he got to it.

Speaking of bridges, he slowly approached the

guard's gate to Figure Eight Island. Panic set in again as to how he was going to explain the half-dead passenger. Ezra hadn't mentioned anything about a guard, but as he got closer, he noticed it was deserted and the gate was left ajar. He cautiously eased the car to a stop, got out, and pulled the gate open the rest of the way. Surveying the area once more before getting back in the car, he shivered. Was it the cool breeze from the ocean or the creepy feeling he was being watched by something in the distance? Either way, he had to Charlie to the house, so he pressed on over the bridge, making the left turn heading up North Beach Street which sent him into an area of darkness running parallel to the coastline. It reminded him of Duck. He continued, trying hard to see what was around him, but the darkness had devoured any signs of anything out here.

"The destination is on your right," GPS blurted out, startling him once more like she'd done pretty much the whole way there. He noticed the turn immediately because it was the first sign of life he'd seen since he got onto the island. It was illuminated by gaslit torches sitting on the top of two square stone columns - one on each side of the drive. *Kind of archaic for my taste.* However, it suited Ezra perfectly.

The house at the end of the drive was another story altogether. A three-story mansion accented with lighted scones at the windows and doors. The white trim stood out the most against what looked like a dark gray or blueish-gray color. The drive led them past the garage and right up to the front entrance of the house.

"Holy shit, Ezra!" he mumbled aloud. "You've been holding out on me."

He exited the car to get a better view, almost forgetting about his incapacitated passenger. Losing himself in the magnificence of the property, he nearly shat himself when Ezra came running out the front door.

"What the hell are you doing here? I thought you were up in Duck taking care of things," Victor started to quiz.

"I did take care of things. I cleaned up the mess you created, drove his car off one of the docks and into the ocean, then changed into a mist and glided down the coastline," Ezra answered, opening the passenger door to get Charlie out. "And I still beat you here. Now, give me a hand."

"Mist," Victor mumbled, throwing his hands up in the air, as he ran to the other side of the car, closing the door behind them. He followed them into the house where he couldn't believe his eyes. Everything was marble - the columns, the floors, the countertops, the stairs. It looked as if he'd walked into a home belonging to an A-listed Hollywood star. He saw Ezra standing in front of a wall and briefly wondered what he was doing, but it became evident he was waiting on him.

"Can you get over here and push this button?" Ezra asked.

"Push a button?" he muttered, then continued towards the two of them. The lighted round circle resembled an elevator button, but there was no way there was an elevator in here. But a few seconds later a secret door within the walls opened into a full-sized elevator that whisked them up to the third floor.

"I can't believe this house. It's freakin' amazing," Victor commented as he ran his fingers across the marble seals of the large porthole-shaped windows overlooking the grounds. "How long have you lived here?"

"I've had this place for some time now. The island used to be full of other dwellers, but as times changed, they moved away one by one, allowing me to snag up their properties and create a private island of my own," Ezra answered as he struggled to get himself and Charlie through a doorway.

"And you're sure you didn't have anything to with them disappearing?" Victor asked hesitantly.

"Unlike you, I properly dispose of my prey," he commented pointedly and smiled briefly before laying Charlie on the bed. "But no. I had nothing to do with them leaving. Cost got too high, interest rates went through the roof, and taxes out the wazoo. It was all economical."

"Sure, if you say so," Victor shot him a side eye and smirk. "And too bad we weren't married. I could have nickel and dimed you for every bit of this."

"Stay here with him. Don't leave his side. When he starts to turn, he's going to need your help. That's when it's time to feed him. Nothing sooner. Do you hear me?" Ezra walked to the edge of the doorway, ignoring his little snide remark.

"Wait where are you going?" he asked, confused. "Are you not going to help me…?"

"Look, I cleaned up the mess and got you a place to stay for a while," he held his head down almost biting down on a fist to his mouth. "I'm going to give the two of you some space. Should another emergency arise, I'll be around to save the day. As I always am."

Victor watched him slowly turn and walk out the door, pulling it closed behind him. He almost spoke up asking him to stay but decided against it. Instead, he pulled up one of the chairs and sat holding Charlie's hand, but it wasn't long before he ditched the chair and crawled into the king-size bed. His body lying next to him - arm wrapped tightly around his waist. The sound of the death rattle breathing filled his ear as he laid his head on his chest. It wasn't long before he fell asleep.

# Chapter Eleven

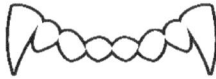

## A New Life...

The sounds of grunting, growling, and pure aggravation woke Victor from his slumber. Charlie's body was fighting a battle within itself. Parts of it dying off, other parts of it becoming an immortally fixed asset of his new journey. This must be it. This must be the time frame Ezra was talking about. He looked at his watch to check the time. He'd slept most of the day and completely lost track of time.

"Here, baby. Here," he said, holding his wrist up to Charlie's mouth. It wasn't long before the canines slid down into fangs, and he felt them pierce the inside of his thin flesh. He flinched a little from the pain but got distracted when he heard the door open. Looking up, he saw Ezra slowly enter the room. What felt like hours had only been minutes before Victor started to feel lightheaded and nearly dropped to his knees. He caught himself on the bed before his body could hit the floor.

"That's enough, Victor," he heard Ezra speak up as Charlie continued to suck the life out of him. "Victor! Stop! Now!"

"I can't get him to let go," he yelled, but in a frantic attempt to release himself, he ripped the thin layer of skin right off his wrist - blood poured onto the bed and floor and Charlie collapsed back into the bed. "Jesus Christ!"

"No, he's not gonna help you," Ezra joked. "Come here." He took Victor's arm and proceeded to wrap the wound with gauze and medical wraps. "It will be healed by morning. Right in time for his next feeding."

"Oh, joy! When does he become self-sufficient?" he asked sarcastically, rubbing and applying pressure to the bandages. He glanced back towards the bed and could see Charlie's body - nearly glowing with life, and the death rattle fading away as his body resurrected. The same life which had been drained from his wrist, his veins…his soul. He could already feel the next feeding deep in his skin. Would there be anything left of him? It was truly a first-time experience. He'd always been the one doing the feeding. Now he felt like a part of him was leaving his undead shell. He needed some time to wrap his mind around it. *Had he gone through this very process when Ezra had turned him? Was this how Ezra felt while he was feeding off of him?* Feelings of compassion flooded over him. He needed an escape. "Where's the bathroom in this place?"

"Soon… and take your pick of any of the six full baths and two half baths. They are halfway up each hallway on the right," Ezra gestured towards the direction. "I'll sit here with him while you go freshen up. Be sure to keep the bite out of the water for now. Don't want to slow the healing."

"Is that even a thing? Don't we heal automatically these days?" Victor raised his eyebrows at him, questioning his own statement, then walked away.

The long hallway eventually turned to the left leading into another wing of the house. The bathroom was conveniently located as he'd said. He walked in to find his and hers - or rather his and his - everything. It was like the bathroom was a whole wing of its own. It even had its own foyer when you entered, splitting into separate "his" sides - each one having a full bathroom of its own. Talk about heaven!

Victor found the towel sets, which appeared never to have been used, hanging on the outside glass shower wall. He reached in and turned the water to the hottest setting. Water started pouring from the multiple shower heads above. As he waited for it to reach the right temp, he took a step back, observing himself in the mirror. He raised his shirt over his head and let it fall to the floor. Taking his unbitten arm and rubbing his hand across his chest, he copped a feel of his own pec before giving himself a wink and dropping trou. But he noticed something different. His reflection had started to fade. He rubbed his eyes, trying to focus his vision, but nothing changed. What did this mean? Ezra must have installed trick mirrors in this place. Something was up or was his existence really being sucked away - one feeding at a time.

He shook off the rising concern dominating his mind and stepped into the shower. The water hit his body from all directions. He let it run down his body while leaning his head back in a relaxed state. The soap and water washed the remaining blood away that'd dried to his body, pooling brownish-red water around the slowly draining grate. Of course, no shower experience would be complete without a few tugs on his manhood. He lathered it up with soap, cupped his low-hanging balls, wrapped his fingers around the base, and gave it a few pumps. It wasn't long before he was at full attention and his fist was pumping and twisting faster and faster. His mind started flashing images of the lighthouse, the beach house, The Cruisy Surf, and any other place he'd spent alone with Charlie. But suddenly, it all switched. He found his mind interjecting images of Ezra until he was the dominant character in his fantasies - the way he took control, the way he protected them, the way he held his arm while wrapping it with bandages. All of it started to make his undead heart beat faster and faster, pumping more undead blood into his already rock-hard organ. It turned him on even more. He tilted his head back, immersed in the intense pleasure of his own hand. He could feel the climax getting close and braced himself against the back wall of the shower. Thrusting his hips forward one final time, it erupted, spewing down his hand and dripping onto the shower floor. Slow deep breaths brought him back into reality. "What the fuck was that?" he said aloud to himself, then once again leaned back against the shower wall, letting the water wash away the remaining mess he'd created.

The thought of Ezra in any light hadn't given him anything but disgust over the past few decades. Now, here he was - back in *his* house - having intense sexual fantasies about him. This was going to make things extremely awkward. He said to himself, "*A lot is going on. It was just a tension release. That's all it was.*" He did his best to brush it all off - the mirror, the fantasies, the questions - while he finished drying off and getting dressed.

On his way back to Charlie, something caught his eye out of one of the five port-hole windows lining the hallway. It was the breathtaking view of the Atlantic Ocean extending indefinitely. Nothing was around them for miles. Ezra had really managed to seclude himself on this island. It really was the perfect place to get away from the hustle and bustle of life - or lack thereof - he guessed. He spotted a large tin pipe sticking up from the sand with steam rising out of it. *Seems kind of odd. Wonder what that is?* But his mind didn't wonder long before he turned away, deciding it was some random house amenity.

Walking back into the bedroom he heard a familiar voice. It gave him the worst feeling of disdain. Tally Atwater was on the wall-mounted television discussing the events of the night before. He wondered what lies she'd be pandering this time.

"It was a complete mess, Kaplin," she dramatized. He noticed she was standing outside the Walmart parking area. "The two victims have been identified as twenty-year-old Leroy Huffman, an engineering student, and forty-five-year-old Gloria Kingston, a single mom to three beautiful young girls. The cause of death has not been released to the public yet, but it was confirmed… there were two fang-like marks on each of the victims' necks."

"Thanks, Tally," Kaplin stared into the camera. "Any updates on closing down the island until this predator is caught?"

"No, Kaplin. As things go now, there is no confirmation on closing the beaches or stopping access to the island, though it has been discussed since the last victim washed ashore." Tally also stood with a fake smile looking into the camera until it panned away to the Walmart building in the background and the ropes of caution tape surrounding the area.

"I should've had you take care of her while you

were at it," Victor said as the television went to a commercial break. "The woman makes my skin crawl."

"Now what good would that have done?" Ezra responded chuckling a bit. "She has no part in this. She's only doing her job. Reporting the news as it happens."

"Maybe, but you've never met her. She's quite pushy, always exaggerates, and is downright annoying." He mimed holding a microphone - flipping his hair from side to side as he impersonated her.

"And how do you like becoming a vampire, sir?" Victor impersonated with his fake microphone stuck in Charlie's blank face. It even managed to raise a smile out of Ezra before he ended his charade and returned back to Charlie's bedside, taking his hand in his. The two remained silent for what seemed like an eternity. The TV creating the perfect background noise as an episode of Golden Girls played. Out of nowhere, Ezra spoke.

"He's doing ok, Vic. He's resting. Let him rest," Ezra said in his best parenting voice. "Come on. You also need to eat. It will help keep your strength up while the transitioning process takes place."

"Is it the reason why I'm fading in the mirrors, or have you turned the bathrooms into some funhouse exhibit?" Victor asked.

"Haha! No. You're fading in the mirrors because

as you transfer life to another being, a part of your life's essence transfers too," Ezra explained. "It's all part of growing as a vampire. Think of it as reaching puberty. Your body starts to change and transition to adulthood. Well… you're finally transitioning to an adulthood."

"Like an adult vampire? That's a thing? I thought once you were turned, you were simply a vampire. You never told me there were different stages," Victor said.

"Yes, there are different stages. Now we can discuss this more when there's time, but we need to get you something to eat. Let's go." Ezra said, rushing him out the door.

"Oh, we're going out? On a hunt? We've not done this together in a while," Victor responded, exiting the bedroom, but as they entered the elevator, he noticed he pushed an unmarked button.

"You're not going anywhere out there. You've created enough of a mess, but however, we *are* going down," he locked eyes with Victor. A smile arose on his face as one of his fangs glistened in the overhead light.

"Going down? Just the way I like it, but what are you? A walking advertisement for teeth whitening?" he joked, playfully punching his shoulder.

The chime of the elevator sounded, and it shakily came to a stop. The door slowly opened into what appeared to be some type of laboratory. Had the elevator taken him to some hidden underground facility? It reminded him of an old video game he used to play some time ago called *Resident Evil. Was this the underground HIVE?* Ezra stepped out first, leading the way into the strange unfamiliar room.

"Welcome to my state-of-the-art lab," he said, arms stretched out and slowly turning in circles as if he was leading a spectacular museum tour as Vanna White. He pressed on, "Each refrigerator is filled with gallons upon gallons of lab-generated synthetic human blood bags. Take your pick." He opened one of the fridges to show the peppermint candy blend of red blood-filled bags and white plastic interior backgrounds.

"Who made all this?" Victor wondered aloud. "Is this even safe to consume?"

"It's perfectly safe for all involved. Well, except for the few prey who have to be used to harvest the platelets from the blood. Everything else is synthetically generated," he explained. "But one prey can provide enough platelets to last around six months, so it drastically reduces the number of times we have to actually hunt."

"Well, damn. There goes the fun out of it," he quipped. "Hey, Ezra. Come on… let's go out tonight. Let's go have some…"

He was cut off by the immediate knee-jerk reaction to catch the bag of red concoction flying at his face. He'd received his answer to going out. But truth be told, the last thing he needed to do was go out a create more of a mess. That's one thing Ezra was right about. This here was a good thing Ezra had going. It was secluded and had its own food supply. There was nothing left to be desired - food, privacy, relaxation - it was all here in this house. Well, maybe a sexy masseur would have been nice. However, he wasn't quite sure there wasn't one hidden around here somewhere.

His face flooded with confusion as he inspected the bag.

"How am I supposed to even drink this? Bite into it?" He flipped the bag around as if searching for a place to insert a straw like it was a Capri-Sun. Man, he hadn't thought about those in years, but the thought of gnawing on this plastic bag was not appealing.

"The luer lock connector serves two functions. For consumption, put your mouth on it and suck it in. If I remember correctly, you're pretty good at that," he replied, shooting side eye and a wink to Victor.

"Really? Okay… well…," He gave the top of the bag one last look. "Bottom's up!"

He tilted his head back, holding the bag in his fist, and sucked in as hard as he could. The taste of the crimson liquid filled his mouth, running down his throat with every gulp. He could fill it immediately revitalizing his every being and the thirst fading away more and more. He tried to see his reflection in the stainless-steel refrigerators, but it was no use. The image was blurred regardless.

"Damn, this shit is da bomb!" He tossed the bag into one of the receptacles. "Can I have some more?"

"All in due time. Our studies have shown, one pouch tends to last around a month and…"

"A month?" Victor said, surprised something synthetic could be so sustainable. "And who's 'our'?"

"What?" Ezra suddenly looked puzzled.

"You said 'our studies'. Who is 'our'?"

"Let's get back to your…"

"No. No. No. Now you're avoiding the question. Why can't you answer me? What are you really doing down here?" He started looking around, flipping through papers on countertops. "Why - all of a sudden - are you acting like you're hiding something?"

"Can't you for once mind your own business?" Ezra snapped back. "I'm trying to help you. I've cleaned up the mess you created, invited you into my home, taken care of you and your play toy, and provided you with food.

Yet, all you can do is stand here and interrogate me. Why? Can't you just be happy with what you have?"

"You know, it was stupid of me to think things could be jovial while getting through whatever process this is," Victor argued, as he moved closer towards him. "The only reason we are here is because you couldn't stand the fact I found someone who made me happy. I was happy. You took the first opportunity to take matters into your own hands and rip that from me... Things were going fine till you decided to come back…"

"Fine? Bodies were washing up on shore. Bodies which you'd sunk your teeth into! And what I did with Charlie was something you couldn't bring yourself to do. I gave him a chance at life. An eternal life so the two of you could be together forever. And this is the thanks I get."

Victor moved in closer, his nose nearly touching Ezra's. His expression said everything. Every bit of aggression channeled into his emotions. They continued to bicker back and forth - in each other's face - as the tension grew between the two. Like a dense fog rolling down the Appalachian Mountains after sunset, it was so thick you could cut it. Suddenly, it all dissipated.

Victor was abruptly interrupted by one of the most surprisingly awkward things that could've happened. Ezra's lips quickly pressed against his own. Not only did it stop him mid-sentence, but it completely took his breath away. How was he supposed to react? Sure, his little moment in the shower may have featured a similar scenario, but he never really expected anything to come of it. He'd already convinced himself of that. But now… right here… this moment, every passionate escapade, along with every red flag, started going off but he gave in as they stared deep into each other's eyes. Victor pounced, wrapping his hands around Ezra's face, pulling him into him, they became one.

Charlie squinted, protecting his eyes from the flashing lights on the television. He looked around as best he could, trying to figure out where he was. At first, he thought maybe it was a hospital, but when he didn't feel any wires or IVs attached to his body or hear beeping machines all around, he ruled that one out. The news was being broadcast - that he was sure of. He recognized Tally Atwater's voice and listened intently as she told her version of the previous night's events. None of it rang a bell, but one thing he did notice was how sonically clear the sounds were. It was a different feeling than he was used to. The blurry vision started to clear, and the view of the vast room opened up. The white walls and expensive-looking furnishings gave the impression that wherever he was, it was well above his means. This must be some sort of dream or a really sick joke. The last thing he remembered was walking up the stairs to the beach house and collapsing on the bed. *Wait… there was something else.* He vaguely remembered running into Victor in the hall. He was covered in blood. *Probably a drunken dream.* But strangely, he could still smell it - the distinct metallic aroma overlaying sea salt. He liked it. It turned him on. He traced the source to what used to be white sheets covering his body. He was covered in it.

It triggered something in him, and the previous night's events flashed before his eyes. Victor in the hallway covered in blood, his entry into the living where a strange man in a fancy suit grabbed him, the piercing needle-like pain on his neck, everything going black as he hit the floor. And now… waking up covered in blood-drenched bed sheets. He felt his neck. It was wrapped in bandages which he frantically ripped off. Things were starting to become clearer as he pulled the duvet up to his face, taking in the aroma. An unfamiliar feeling ran through his body - a sense of power, a sense of godliness, a sense of thirst.

He tossed the covers back, quickly leaping out of the bed and landing perfectly on all fours. *Wow! That was fast.* He stood upright, stretching every muscle in his body and realizing he was definitely more flexible than he used to be. Finding the door slightly ajar, he cautiously exited the room - the long hallway was his to explore. No one was in sight. He wandered down the hallway, opening doors here and there expecting to find someone along the way.

Nothing. And no one. He was alone. The line of porthole windows caught his attention, and he peered out the first one he came to. He could see the ocean. That explained the sea salt, but this wasn't the beach house. *Where the hell am I?* He noticed a lower section of the house with bright fluorescent lights emitting from the window. The steam rising from the pipe next to them blocked the view, but he could have sworn he saw someone moving around down there. But how could he get there was the question? And where was Victor? Where was anyone for that matter?

He continued to roam the halls until he'd almost come full circle back to the room when he noticed the small round button on the wall. He pushed it because that's what you do to random buttons on a wall. At first, nothing happened. Suddenly, he heard a loud ding sending a ringing in his ears and taking him to his knees. Holding his hands over his ears, he looked up as the wall was splitting apart to reveal the elevator. The buttons inside lined the wall to the right of the door - three, two, one, and blank. He didn't know where he was going, but from the view out the window, he'd already figured out there were more than three floors to whatever this building was. He pushed the blank one and hoped for the best.

# Chapter Twelve

## Heartbreak...

Charlie covered his ears in preparation for the loud ding as the elevator came to a stop and the doors pulled apart. The refrigerator-filled room came into view. He immediately thought of food. When was the last time he'd eaten anything? He opened one of the double-doored fridges, not noticing the label on the top: *WARNING! NOT FOR CONSUMPTION!* Inside he found bags and bags of red liquid. instantly triggering a thirst he couldn't control. The fangs dropped and he ripped into the bags one after the other. A surge of adrenaline passed through his body. It was better than any orgasm he'd ever experienced – including with Victor. He basked in this new glory, resting against one of the counters in the center of the room till being ripped out of the bliss by a commotion in the back room.

He got up, heading toward the door. The closer he got, the more his senses became alert - pulses rushing, heavy breathing, loud moaning, the strong scent of something familiar - but when he opened the door, it was like someone had driven a stake right through his heart. The noises were coming from two people in the heat of deep passionate sex. One lying on top of a desk - their legs held up in the air. The other, drilling his manhood deep into his mate. They stopped and looked at him like deers in the headlights of a car. Right away, he recognized them. One was the love of his life. The other was the one who took his life… well some form of it at least.

"Oh shit!" he heard, watching Victor push the other one away and slide off the desk, scrambling for his clothes, saying – unbelievably: "Babe, what are you doing out of bed? You should be resting. You're gonna need your strength."

Apparently, he was oblivious to the fact he was caught fucking someone else. Charlie's anger boiled and a loud growl filled the room. His eyes turned as crimson as the blood that once ran through his body - fangs out and ready to fight.

"Okay… Okay… I get it. You're upset. I was too, at first," Victor said, struggling to get his pants on. "Let's go sit down and talk. We can talk about this. It's going to be ok. I'll help you..."

Charlie picked up the chair sitting by the door and line drove it towards his head. Ezra flung his arm into the air and the chair stopped mid-flight.

"Enough!" he yelled, and the chair hit the floor.

"Charlie, baby, I'm so sorry," Victor pleaded, slowly moving closer.

"What did you do? Who the hell is this? Why the fuck are you fucking him, and what did he do to *me*?" he angrily quizzed. Flashes of his mother's interrogations ran through his mind.

"Well, it's quite a long story. You see..."

"Tell me!!" Charlie interrupted. This time though something changed within him. His words had turned more into a roar that shook the entire contents of the room. His eyes now changed from red to a red pupil surrounded by a golden ring. He could feel the bones in his body starting to bend and conform into a different position. "You lied to me!"

"Baby, I'm sorry. A lot has happened in the past forty-eight hours or so, and we really need to sit down and talk," Victor explained. "I really need you to try and calm down, though. This here. This was nothing. An act of pure tension... I can't even stand him. He's my ex..."

Charlie felt more cracking of bones inside of him as his anger increased even more and his body started to morph. His nose and mouth started to grow into a snout. His fingernails extended into sharp pointy claws. He cut him off again to continue the interrogation. "What the fuck did this bastard do to me?"

"Well, to answer, there's something I need to explain…"

"Answer me, now!" Charlie yelled. His body was now covered in coarse hair and pointy wolf-like ears stuck up from the top of his head.

"Okay. Okay. The short answer is…" There was a brief pause before Victor actually got the words out. "He turned you into a vampire. He turned me as…"

"Victor! Move! Now!" Ezra shouted, but before anyone could make a move, Charlie's body had completed its morph, ripping away his clothes, and growling furiously in anger. He took a giant leap forward over Victor's head, pouncing around the room and back out the door. Shattering glass hit the floor as he jumped through the window. Perching on the highest peak of the roof, he let out a howl.

"What the fuck was that? That definitely was not a vampire!" Victor yelled. "What just happened?"

"Well, you see… you," Ezra pointed to him, "got caught cheating. And that??? Hmmm… If I had to guess, I'd say the love of your life is now a lycan…and a vampire…a hybrid of sorts."

"I'm sorry… a what?"

"A hybrid. It would explain the enhanced strength, reflexes, coordination, speed, agility, durability, endurance, regenerative abilities, and the shape-shifting that occurred before he pounced around the room and broke my damn window. Is there some other secret about this boy? Was he a wolf and that's why you never turned him?"

"Wait, you're telling me Charlie is now a shapeshifter? And no! No other special secrets I was aware of! How is that even possible?" Victor quizzed. "If you're the only one who bit him and I'm the only one who's fed him, that can't be."

Victor watched Ezra pick his shirt up off the floor and walk into the other room.

"I think I may have found the answer to one of your questions as to how," Ezra yelled from the other room. "It seems your boy helped himself to one of our latest experiments."

"There you go with 'our' again!" He ran over inspecting the open refrigerator and the mess of empty blood bags on the floor. "What exactly was in this thing and why does it say, 'do not consume?'"

"Werewolf blood."

"Excuse me! What?" Victor was starting to get pissed again. As usual, anytime Ezra was around shit hit the fan. No matter how much he may or may not have sexual feelings for him, this was about to be the icing on the cake. "What the hell are you doing with werewolf blood?"

"It's an experiment we're working on. Don't worry about the why. At this point, we need to worry about the where." Ezra was gazing out of the broken window, trying to spot the wolf-like creature. "If he gets off this island, we're in bigger trouble than a few bodies washing up on shore."

"I swear, you rotten piece of shit! How did I let you get back into my life? You've had this planned all along. haven't you? You didn't wanna help me! You needed us to be your little guinea pigs!" Victor shouted from across the room.

"Enough," Ezra said, "What's done is done. Tracking is what we must focus on right now. We need to track him."

"I'm not playing any more of your little games until you explain all of this to me." He stood there, angrier than he'd ever been. "Why were you harvesting werewolf blood?"

"Okay. We were harvesting the blood so we could breed a hybrid creature, more powerful than all of us combined," Ezra explained. "The trial was supposed to start next week, but it looks like it's going to start sooner. Do keep in mind though, I am not the one who went wandering into my refrigerators looking for food."

"Oh, for fuck's sake, of course!" Victor threw his hands in the air. "You're not responsible for any of this. Why wasn't it locked? What do you have to combat this? How do you plan to keep him on the island?"

He didn't give Ezra a chance to respond. The rapid fire of queries blurted out as each one came to mind. There were now so many unanswered questions. One's even he knew Ezra couldn't answer. Why hadn't he stayed by his side instead of leaving him alone? What would be the outcome of their relationship now? It was surely over now. He felt a hand on his shoulder.

"Pull yourself together. It's gonna be ok," Ezra

assured. "Think about it this way, now you can get into pup play. With your very own pup." He chuckled at himself. "But with all seriousness, there are plans in place to keep the subjects on the island. Most of the area is fenced along the perimeters of the island facing the mainland. I truly hope they work. We've never had one out in the wild."

"I need you to tell me how to capture him so I can sit him down and talk to him. I can make any of this better if I can talk to him," he pleaded.

"Now, now," Ezra said, patting him on the shoulder. "That pretty smile and impeccable persuasion will no longer work with him. He'll see right through it. You're going to have to level with him one-on-one. Be truthful. Because if you're not, he'll know."

"But how do I subdue him so I can level with him?" Victor pleaded.

"Give him some time to calm down. He'll change back soon enough," Ezra said. "Hell, he may even come back. Wouldn't that be wonderful?"

"Why are you such a smart ass?" he said, pressing the button to leave the laboratory and enter the elevator to the main floor, leaving Ezra to clean up the mess in the lab.

"It's part of my charm, I guess," he replied with a flashing smart-elec smile.

Victor glared at him as the elevator doors closed. Any feelings of sexual tension or attraction to him had completely diminished and he needed to get out of this house, away from him, and to someplace where he could gather his thoughts. Unfortunately, there was nothing on this godforsaken island.

The elevator dinged and the doors opened onto the main floor. Victor exited and started to explore. He was only in this room for a moment when he'd arrived, but surely there was someplace he could go.

The expansive patio was off to the right of the fully marbled and stainless-steel kitchen. guarded by two sets of full-length French doors. He swung one side of them open and walked out onto the patio. It spanned the entire length of the house and was filled with tables, chairs, lounge chairs, couches surrounding a gas fire pit, and a large infinity pool at the far end. There was an extended walkway taking him down to the beach.

The island was quiet except for the sounds of waves crashing against the shoreline. He stood there for a moment looking out at the sea. Memories played in his mind of him and Charlie walking down the beach, sitting outside the lighthouse, the first time he took Charlie to the house in Duck. He started walking. He didn't know where he was heading - but damnit! - he knew he had to do something until he came up with a plan. First, to explain to Charlie how they'd made it to this point. To explain how sorry he was for his actions, and for bringing him into the craziness of life as a vampire. Secondly, getting the two of them off this damn island.

He started running. A slight jog at first then picking up the pace.

Second, a plan to figure out what the hell Ezra was really up to. Why he was planning to breed hybrids, and hopefully, how the two of them could combat it. Who was he working for, or better yet, who was working for him? Who was "our"?

His ran faster.

Third, a plan to move forward should none of this pan out. He was always the pessimist. Planning for things that didn't need to be planned for. Things that would never happen, but he'd be prepared for them if they did. However, this was one situation he hadn't even thought about happening. *How was he going to fill his time now? He didn't need to feed every day. Though, if he left the area, would Ezra continue to allow access to the synthetic food chain? Did he even want to continue that relationship?* He'd have to figure that one out later or at least within the next month.

Faster and faster.

Where the hell was he? He'd probably run around this island eight times by now and nothing was coming to him - each time passing the house - replaying the same things in his mind. Finally, it all came to a halt - literally. His exhausted body gave out and collapsed to the ground.

The impact of his undead flesh hitting the sand hurt like hell, but not as much as the pain in his unsanctified heart. He lay there for a moment before pulling himself up and sitting in the sand. Staring out over the ocean, the remnants of hard waves rushing up against him then quickly, rushing back out to sea. He didn't care. He buried his face in his arms and let out a loud scream. It felt good. It felt like a release he'd never known before. The tears began to flow. He tried to hold them in but there was no use. He was sobbing uncontrollably. What did he care? There was no one there to see him anyway. He'd stay here for as long as it took. This spot. Right here. And when Charlie wanted to see him, he'd find him.

# Chapter Thirteen

## Darkness With Light…

Charlie awoke in a small patch of a wooded area next to an old, abandoned house. His body had morphed back into human form. He lay there, processing the events, starting to release his emotions and come to terms with the changes taking place in his body. So he was a vampire. Okay… how would one explain the whole changing to a wolf aspect that'd just occurred? The feelings he felt when seeing Victor being plowed by someone else obviously set it off. But right now, how was he supposed to control his anger and emotions? There were so many things he was angry about at that moment. What was he going to tell his mother? *Oh hey, Mom! Remember how you wanted your son to be a murderer instead of a queer? How about a human-eating monster? Well, you got your wish, I guess.* Yeah, that wouldn't go over well.

On the bright side, so many things were starting to make sense between him and Victor as he tried to clear his head. The secrets, the lack of food, the big empty house, the escape from the lighthouse, the bodies. He thought hard about the fact that if Victor *was* the one killing these people and disposing of them in the Atlantic, he must have really meant something special to him. There were many opportunities where he could have taken him out and tossed him away. But he hadn't.

He started to shiver as a cool breeze brushed against his body and he discovered he was naked, lying on a patch of grass under one of the trees. He looked around the wooded area to see if anyone was around. But like inside the house, he found himself alone. It was quiet except for the sounds of the ocean in the distance. *They'd surely be coming for him.* But he decided to venture out and at least find some clothes.

He wandered up to one of the nearby houses. The door was wide open, but even with multiple cars in the driveway, no one appeared to be home.

"Hello!" he yelled out, but there was no answer.

The house was big enough to be a castle, as were most of the houses in the area. He entered and quickly learned whoever lived here or used to live here must have left in a hurry because the house was in complete disarray. He went through it searching for anything of use. They must have had a teenage boy - two for that matter, because there was a twin-sized bed on each side of the room. The clothes in one of the closets looked like they'd come directly from an Abercrombie store. He thought about how the chain had been in business for years making money off all the teeny-bopper college kids or those in their thirties and forties wishing they were still in their late teens or twenties. Not really his style, but it'd work as long as they covered his naked ass. But before he put on any clothes, he would need to clean up a bit. Between the dripping blood dried to his chin, turning into a wolf-like creature, and lying naked in the dirt he'd gotten pretty nasty. Not to mention he reeked of wet dog.

He found the bathroom to be an ornate room with enough amenities to put the Hilton hotel chain to shame. Turning on the sink faucet, he was shocked to find the house's water supply was still turned on. Even the electricity still worked. *Strange. But if you're going to play the role of Goldilocks, you might as well do it in style.* He turned on the water to the spa-like tub and climbed in. As it filled and the jets started to push the water around, he found himself in a state of relaxation he hadn't felt in a long time. *I could get used to this.*

He reached for the bottle of bodywash left on the side of the tub and scrubbed the dried, crusted blood off his face, neck, and chest. A painful sting ran up his arm as the soap got into one of the cuts he'd accrued while jumping out of the window and he dipped it in the water to quickly rinse it off. Once he felt he was clean enough and the smell of wet dog had been taken over by the lavender scent body wash he got out. The luxury towels hanging on the wall seemed almost too good to use, but he quickly grabbed one and started drying off. The soft plushness absorbed every drop of water as it rubbed across his body.

He searched the cabinets for a first aid kit or some kind of bandage to wrap his arm in. *Where did these people go?* He opened the linen closet - and there, stacked on the shelf were a collection of kits. They had about twenty sitting on a shelf. *They must be apocalyptic savers. Too bad it didn't help them.* It was crazy he'd had the thought because that's exactly what this place felt like. Empty. Deserted. No one to be found.

He got dressed with the clothes he'd picked out from the teens' closet and walked back downstairs to the living room. As he perused the family pictures sitting on the mantle and hanging on the wall, he noticed there was an alarm system at the front door. *Hmmm. Alarm systems these days have cameras.* He looked up to spot one in the corner of the living room ceiling. Since there was still power in the house, Charlie decided to go searching for the monitor systems.

Going from room to room, he finally found a computer in the office on the third floor. Booting it up, he was thankful it wasn't password-protected. He simply had to move the mouse and it lit up like Tokyo. The application for the alarm was on the desktop so he clicked on it to see if it would open. It did. It was almost like they wanted someone to find this. It was way too easy.

The camera system was set to only record when it sensed motion in the area. *This should be easy.* He opened the last file recorded and saw it was him entering the house. *Oh great! They have a permanent record of Goldilocks.* He clicked the next file, which was a lady locking the front door. The same lady he'd recently seen in the photos downstairs, and the door was the one he'd entered through an hour or so ago.

The file continued to play as he watched each of the family members get ready for bed - the mom, dad, and two teenage boys. The time stamp read 05/21/2082 09:21 PM. *Poor kids. They don't even get the privacy to be typical teenage boys.* The file went blank on each of the cameras and the lights were turned out, but at 12:00 AM they flipped back on. Charlie noticed the front door swing wide open and a group of five people enter the house dressed in black robes with torches in their hands.

Entering the boys" room, two of the robed strangers passed their torches to the others and leaned over the boys' beds, appearing to bite down on the crease of their necks. The boys could be seen struggling, kicking, and fighting with all their teenage might until they slowly gave up and succumbed to their fate. *Too bad these things didn't record sound.* The two rose back to an upright position and the boys appeared to be lifeless. Turning on the light, the mom entered the room. The shock of strangers in her house – two of them now covered in teenage ichor, and the boys' apparent fates could be seen on her face. One of the intruders chased her down into the living room where she received the same atrocity as the boys.

The father, on the other hand, was nowhere to be seen. Charlie watched each member of the sinister group go from room to room searching for the missing man. He noticed them pointing to and looking out of a broken window in the bedroom. Distracted by the window, they apparently failed to notice the beast which had entered the room from one of the lavish closets in the master bedroom. Its eyes glowed yellow in the dark room. It jumped at one of the men, taking him down and ripping out his throat with its teeth. The others turned, pushing their torches close to its face. As they kept the animal distracted, a sixth person came out of nowhere and stabbed the beast with a shiny metallic stake. It fell to the floor. *Silver. So cliché.*

One of the guys picked up the beast's body and carried it out, while the others gathered the rest of the family and walked out the door with them in tow. The mysterious sixth person remained in the house cleaning up the messes - cleaning up the blood stains and removing and changing bed sheets so it would appear the family had merely vanished in a hurry. But as he exited the house, he did one thing that was unexpected. He looked right at the living room camera, smirked, and winked before going and leaving the door wide open.

"Oh shit! That's the guy from the house!" Charlie said aloud, as he quickly closed down the program and jumped back from the computer. It was like he knew someone would find this and watch it. His first thought was to find Victor - *old habits die screaming, I guess* - but he had to admit it was going to be on the roster at some point. If this guy is out here taking out families, something must be done to stop him. And it was probably safe to assume he's the reason there's not another human being in sight because this whole island felt like it crawled right out of some classic apocalyptic movie.

It was time to find some protection. He went through the house looking for anything he could find - a bat, kitchen knife, gun, a garden hoe - anything that could be of use. The only thing he found here was a bat and a backpack. *It'll work for now.* He stuffed the backpack with a couple of first aid kits from the bathroom. If the other inhabitants of the island had reached the same fate, then he was bound to find some other useful items in some of the other houses too - though some stakes would probably be a handy item to have around. *Doubt they will just be lying around.*

He left this house and headed to the one next door. The same scenario occurred: door wide open, no one around. He searched around for useful items, this time at least he found a sheriff's belt filled with handcuffs, a taser, a flashlight, a Leatherman multi-tool, and a Glock 22. How sad this officer may have suffered the same fate. He suddenly thought back to Officer Johnny. He felt some odd connection to him now as he put on the belt. *Wonder which one of them was the wolf?* After locating a box of ammo inside the nightstand, he stuffed it into the backpack.

Still rummaging through one of the closets, his newly hypersensitive ears heard a scream in the far distance across the island. It pierced his ears the way a siren would to a dog. He immediately recognized the sound of the voice as Victor's. *Was he hurt? Had they gotten to him?* He took off running towards the noise.

He was starting to adjust to this wolf thing. The heightened senses made for a good tool in itself for defense, but in this case, it would also lead him straight to Victor. He took a good deep breath and headed towards a familiar scent.

On his journey across the island, he reminisced. Now understanding how Victor was able to run so fast the night they were out on the beach - the night before shit really started to hit the fan. He wished he could go back to that night - the two of them, walking along the beach, hanging out in front of the lighthouse in each other's arms. Life before it got so complicated so quickly.

He slowed down before reaching the most remote part of the island, surveying the area before exposing himself to the open landscape. There didn't seem to be anything obviously alarming. His target, however, was sitting straight ahead in the sand, waves rushing up on him, head down on his folded arms.

Charlie slowly walked out of the wooded area and onto the open beach. There was a trench, appearing to curve around the island as if someone's path had sunk in. Victor was sitting right in the middle of it. Charlie was glad to see he wasn't hurt, and this would give him a chance to fill him in on the things he'd seen. He quietly strolled up and said, "Hey!... Is this sand taken?"

# Chapter Fourteen

## The Rekindling…

"What?" Victor looked up. The sun was blinding, but he obviously knew the voice.

"Can I sit down?" Charlie asked.

"Yes, please," he answered. "Listen, I'm so sorry. I never wanted to get you involved in all this vampire stuff."

"I'd have figured it out when I was seventy-four and you still looked like you were in your late twenties," Charlie joked.

"True. Wait… you would have hung around that long?"

"I realize now, if you wanted to eat me, you would

have," he continued.

"Well, I did kinda eat you… a few times, actually," Victor smiled, trying to lighten the mood.

"Okay, you got me there, but you know what I mean," Charlie replied. "Listen, we've got a lot to unpack. I'm not gonna lie, but all in all, I'm coming to terms with things within myself. Just don't piss me off again or I'll go all wolfangster on you again."

"Please don't ever say that again!" Victor laughed and laid his head on Charlie's shoulder. "But listen, I'm willing to put in the work if you're still willing to."

"Good! Cause we've got work to do," Charlie said. "Your little fuck buddy is not all he seems to be. Vampire, yes. But he's up to something, and we need to get to the bottom of it."

"I was talking about us…,"

"Oh, we're good for now, but you're gonna help me get this bastard. You've not seen the things I've seen in the last couple days. Speaking of… How long have you been sitting out here? Your hands are pruned," he picked up one of Victor's wrinkled paws to show him.

"I'm not really sure. I started walking, then jogging, then running. I didn't know where to go to clear my mind, so I kept going. I tripped … or maybe my body gave out…

I don't know, but at one point I fell. I haven't gotten back up since. But I've not been out here long I don't think... Maybe I lost track of the days. I think I ran longer than I've been sitting, or maybe it's the other way around, but I knew - or at least hoped - if I stayed in one place it would be easier for you to find me."

"I definitely appreciate that 'cause I'm trying to stay incognito on this island," Charlie said. "Apparently, I'm a hot commodity on this little piece of land along with my wolf brothers and sisters."

"What are you talking about? Wolf brothers and sisters? What have you seen?"

"Your little boy toy along with his minions are - or were - out here feasting on the residents of this island." Charlie also told him about the empty houses and the alarming footage he watched on the computer screen.

"That bastard! He told me all these people moved away due to economic issues," Victor replied. "Let's get one thing straight, too, before we continue. He's not my boy toy. He's my ex. He's the person who made me around a hundred years ago. That's all he is. Tensions got high and shit happened this week. That's all it was."

"I get it. It happens and people make mistakes. I'm not a heartless asshole, but I've got it in for the motherfucker now. They murdered kids. Or at least that's what seemed to have happened. Maybe they have them locked up somewhere, turning them as well. Grooming them for something."

"A war."

"What?" Charlie asked. "What did you say?"

"A war. He told me he was building hybrids. Which is what you now are - part vampire, part wolf - to be more powerful than all the others," Victor explained.

"So, I'm the most powerful beast in all the lands," Charlie stopped and thought for a moment, letting a little bit of arrogance get to his head. "We can definitely use this to our advantage."

"Don't let it go to your head, but there's another thing. he says supposedly fences are blocking off the island from the mainland. I haven't seen them. Maybe they are invisible? Maybe they are underground? I don't know," Victor said.

"That explains why there is still power to most of this island. He needs it to generate the fences," Charlie said. "Listen, I don't think they can affect me - like shock-wise. I'm not wearing any kind of device or collar. The most they can do is keep us from getting out, but if we can find out where those fences are located, we could disable them to be safe. Truth be told, though, these houses are pretty damn awesome. Not sure I want to get out. I could stay here, you know. After we take out the vampire lord and all his minions."

"You'd just pack up and leave your family? What about your mom?" Victor asked.

"Whelp, there comes a time when you have to cut certain people out of your life. They do more harm than good. Sometimes that includes blood relatives. It's sad, but it has to happen. Family can sometimes be the most toxic," Charlie paused for a moment, changing the subject. "Yeah, so which house are we picking as headquarters? I found a wonderful castle on the south side of the island."

"Technically, I'm family now. You haven't cut me yet?" Victor looked up and him. "And I've been pretty toxic."

"Jesus, man! Would you stop playing the Bella Swan here?" he replied. "You're giving me straight out of an early 2000s vibe here and it's dampening my mood."

"Hold up. You know who that is?" Victor asked, a surprised look on his face. "Now were going back to my really early days."

"Do not go all sparkly on me," Charlie joked.

"I can make it happen. I did it with glitter one time. I'm sure there's a Dollar Store somewhere around here where we could pick up some up," Victor smiled. "I used to love glitter. It was the make-up of my childhood."

"Don't you dare!" Charlie snapped back quickly, cutting him a side-eye glance.

The two of them sat in silence for a while watching the ocean, arms around the other, taking in the moment. Victor let their conversation sink in. The two of them together, fighting vampires. Who'd have thought? He knew at one point they'd have to get into the nitty-gritty of things, but for now, all was right in the world… at least for his world.

"You know, you seem like you've become more assertive since all this took place," Victor said. "What happened to the meek guy who visited The Cruisy Surf for the first time?"

"Oh, he's dead. He died in that bed a couple days ago," he replied. "The person who rose up is who I am now, and I've embraced that. I haven't figured out where the wolf part came into play."

"That one is mostly on you. The fridge you broke into was filled with Ezra's stockpile of werewolf blood," Victor explained. "The mixture of my blood and the blood in the pouches during the early stages of transitioning blended together to create the hybrid. The anger and adrenaline of seeing…yeah… caused it to kick in even faster."

"That's simple enough, I guess. Truth be told, I kinda like it. Except smelling like a wet dog," Charlie replied. "Oh, and having to find new clothes every time the transition happens. That's going to be a pain. I found myself naked under a tree the other day."

"Naked under a tree, you say," Victor smirked. "Sounds hot."

"Yeah? You think?" Charlie smiled.

"You're still the most attractive person I've seen in the last… oh a hundred years," he answered, rubbing the top of his head.

They leaned in for a kiss. First, a soft touch of each other's lips, then tongues slipping in and out, tangling with each other's. Passion took its toll and Victor felt Charlie's new-found dominance take control. He lay back into the sand as Charlie climbed on top of him, the water rushing up against them with each incoming wave.

"I'm taking the wheel this time," he heard him say as he straddled his waist and pulled his shirt over his head exposing his washboard-flat abs now appearing even more perfect with his new-found transformation. He looked down as Charlie grabbed ahold of his shirt and ripped it off. He pulled him down, bare chest to bare chest, they touched. Victor could feel the sweet caress of Charlie's lips on his forehead, moving down to his right ear, and then slowly down his neck. The immense pleasure was mixed with a little bit of pain as he felt two sharp fangs lightly pierce the skin and the flow of warm liquid run down his neck. Charlie rose up. The blackish, crimson liquid ran down his chin as Victor watched him tilt his head back in ecstasy. He felt him rise up from his waist and flip him over in one swoop.

The sense of not being in control was something Victor hadn't experienced in a long time. It was pure pleasure as he let himself give way to Charlie's desires. At this moment he could have ripped his throat out and he wouldn't have cared. He buried his face in his arms to keep from grinding it into the sand, rising to breathe with each wave crashing in. He felt Charlie lift his waist off the ground – pulling his shorts down his legs – then mounted him. He heard something hit the sand above his head. He looked up and saw it was a pair of tan shorts equipped with a kit belt.

"I'm gonna fuck you like the animal you are," he heard him whisper in his ear.

"You want this? Yeah?"

"Yeah, I want it!" he was immediately pulled back into the heat of the action and released every tense muscle in his body as Charlie slid into him. It hurt at first, but with each thrust - harder and harder - the pain turned to pleasure. Charlie lifted him off the sand, bringing him to his knees and elbows. The pup submitting to his master. He rose up, leaning back into him as he felt Charlie's hand reach around and grab his throbbing piece. *Thrust thrust.* His body was now moving in sync with every move.

He tilted his head back, his lips tasting himself as they brushed against the blood-covered face of his subduer. *Thrust thrust.* He let out a deep moan and could feel himself getting closer to release. Charlie deep inside him. The saltwater of the sea crashing again the two of them. He couldn't take it anymore. His whole body shivered with pure bliss as his rock-hard member exploded onto the sand. *Faster faster. Thrust thrust. Harder harder.* He felt Charlie give one last push deep into him and heard him let out a moan that almost sounded like a howl. The two collapsed on the sand, Charlie on top, still inside him.

They both caught their breaths, lying there taking in the essence of sex. Charlie rolled off him and he rolled over. The two of them exposed to the world.

"Damn, that was good!" Victor said, still catching his breath. "I think I'm going to like this new you."

"Me too," Charlie said, chuckling.

"I'm gonna need a new shirt though."

"Sorry. But I'm pretty sure I know where you can get another one," Charlie replied. "There are tons of empty houses sitting around on this island. Let's wash up though and get a move on. I'm dead meat if they catch me out here in the open."

"Speaking of… where'd you find the kit belt and gun?" Victor asked.

"I found it in another one of the victim's houses," he answered. "Figured it would come in handy."

"Nice. Well, not really under the circumstances, but nice for us at the moment," Victor remarked.

The two dipped into the ocean to rinse the ecstasy off their naked bodies before dressing and heading back into the woods, concealed from the open view.

"I'm curious, though. How do you think we are going to find a layout of these fences?" Victor asked.

"Oh, I'm not. You are! You're going back in."

# Chapter Fifteen

## A Plan in Place...

Ezra stood peering out one of the porthole windows.

"I told you he got out!" he exclaimed to the person on the other end of the phone.

"I had the warning labels on the fridge. Not my fault he didn't read them. Get your ass over here. Now! Gather the others as well. We're going to need to hunt this motherfucker down if we want to continue this little experiment."

He ended the call wishing he could have slammed the phone down loud enough for whoever on the other end to hear it. Those were the good ol' days. The plan was falling apart. He never thought of how letting Victor and his little prey into his house would create such a mess. Which was sad because he normally thought of everything. Everything was always planned out strategically. One little moment of weakness and everything is now on the verge of falling apart.

He entered the elevator, but this time before selecting a floor, he pressed a small button on his gold ring - something he'd always worn. The button released the top portion of the ring turning it into a key which he inserted into a keyhole on the elevator's control panel. Turning the key, a small latch flipped up revealing another button. He pushed it, closed the flap, and removed the key. The elevator continued down past the lab then came to a shivering stop.

The doors opened onto a dark room - filled with the potent aroma of feces - which was illuminated by round red emergency lights on the walls. He flipped a switch allowing fluorescent lighting to fill the room. The sounds of others cringing at the lights could be heard, as well as loud banging on the jail-like cages filled the room.

"Oh, zip it!" he said. "I'm not here to feed you. You'll be lucky if you ever get fed again if you keep this up."

He took a metal pole and clanged it against the bars

as if taunting the herd of people gathered like sheep in cages. There was one in particular he was looking for amongst the crowd.

"Get back!"

He opened a cage, corralling them towards the back, some forced to stand on the single toilet meant to be used by the twenty or so people locked in this Jail-like cell. Locating his subject, he grabbed a young man by the collar which had been placed around his neck, dragging him out and tossing him down on the floor. A woman screamed, "No, not my baby. Take me!" but he ignored her cries. Once he'd locked back up, he hoisted the guy onto a gurney and began strapping him down. He was fairly subdued and didn't put up much of a fight.

Ezra walked around to a monitoring system in the center of the room next to the gurney and typed a few things into the keyboard. It seemed to come to life with robotic arms moving into place - each arm lowering towards the guy's body.

He walked over and adjusted the placement a bit with one facing the throat and the other into a bicep. Pressing the enter key to lock them into place allowed for two long needles to appear from inside the arms. They slowly moved closer, entering the subject's body barely enough to draw blood. He flinched as they pierced his skin. The glass tank began to fill with a darkish-red liquid. Ezra punched a few more buttons. then walked back to the elevator. Flipping the lights off, he threw a smirk at the others as the doors closed.

Victor and Charlie were hiding in the bushes outside Ezra's house when they observed a caravan of black Suburban vehicles pull into the driveway and up to the front door. Victor's car was nowhere to be seen. They watched intently as the drivers got out of each vehicle and walked around to the passengers' side to open the doors. It was almost in unison, as if it had been rehearsed.

One by one, people in black hooded robes filed out of the back seats. They formed a straight line before marching up to the front door.

"What are these people? Some kind of cult?" Charlie asked.

"I don't know. I've never seen them before. And what the fuck did he do with my car?" Victor replied.

"Shhhhhhh. You'll get us caught," Charlie snapped back.

The men stopped short of the front door, and Ezra appeared to welcome them in. They each entered the house, bowing before him before crossing the threshold -

like he was some sort of god standing before them. Ezra looked around the perimeter before going in and closing the door behind him.

"What are we going to do now?" Charlie asked. "They didn't say a word, so we have no clue what they are doing in there."

"I have an idea, but you're gonna have to stay here. Give me the multi-tool," Victor replied. "And you hear me? Stay here."

"Yes, sir!" Charlie responded with a mock salute after handing him the tool.

Victor jumped up and ran behind the house. He climbed up onto the back porch and peered through the French doors. He could see the men piling into the elevator. He checked to see if they were unlocked. The doorknob turned perfectly. He slyly entered the house and slipped into the kitchen area. He opened both fridge doors searching for any kind of food, but he was out of luck. *Guess we can't have blood lying around everywhere.* He closed the fridge and turned down the hallway with no clue where he was going.

The hallway led to several rooms on each side. The bathroom was in its usual center of the hall position. Most of the rooms were unlocked with either nothing in them or filled with elaborate bedroom décor like the ones upstairs - mostly, for show. Even now, Ezra was still a fake. Who knows what kind of power trip he was on with these robed people? Victor continued down the hall till he came to a door that was locked. *Wonder what's in here?* He pulled out the multi-took and looked for something small enough to insert into the round keyhole. It took a few tries but finally, he found a piece of the bottle opener that fit perfectly into the lock. Maneuvering it around a few times caused the lock to release and he turned the knob.

The door revealed a room with red walls and white trim. A large desk sat in the center. More porthole windows looked over the back end of the patio. *Hmmm... now why would he need to keep this locked?* He entered the room and quietly closed the door behind him.

Victor searched for anything that might tell him about the strange men dressed in the dark robes, or better yet, what was really going on in this house. Whatever it was, he was ready to take it on. This bitch has been in control of people for long enough - five hundred years too long.

He found nothing of use in the bookcases lining the walls except old books. Great titles though. There was a copy of *The Da Vinci Code* which he'd enjoyed when it came out. *The better read was The Templar Revelation on which it was based.* Ezra seemed like someone, though, who would be into secret societies. Especially after the little charade out in the driveway. *He's got these people eating out of his hand, I bet.* He briefly thought about Charlie and hoped he was ok, but remembered he could probably now handle his own issues should they arise.

Victor rounded the corner of the desk and noticed there was a drawer ajar. He pulled it open and inside sat his car keys along with Charlie's. *I swear if the bastard drove my car into the ocean…* He quickly put them in his pocket and checked the drawer for anything else useful. Nothing. He pulled out each of the other drawers, finding mostly junk and random office supplies until he came across the locked filing drawer. He pulled out his handy dandy multi-tool and whispered aloud, "Don't fail me now." and began looking for a piece to unlock it.

After multiple attempts with various tools, it seemed that nothing was going to get this drawer open. However, the letter opener became quite useful when he jabbed it between the drawer and the desk and gave it a bit too strong of a pull, falling back onto the floor. *Damn vampire strength.* But the drawer was open. The lock was broken, so eventually, Ezra would find out someone had been in there, but nonetheless, it was open.

The large drawer contained many files, all labeled with tabs. He figured they were probably false - decoys to what was actually in them. He flipped through each one until he came across a map of the island stuffed in between some invoices. The Figure Eight Island map consisted of red marker outlines with larger X's in various places around the island. He folded the map and stuffed it into his pocket.

He assumed this could be the location of the fences, but there was really no indication this was what it was. Even so, it would be useful to know they could properly navigate the island.

He continued looking - more invoices - one for a harvester. *What the hell was that?* The product description mentioned something about medical equipment. *Maybe this was used to create the synthetic blood?* He was puzzled for a moment but tossed it back into a folder. Didn't seem like there was anything of use in there, so he closed up the drawer as best he could and exited the office, locking it behind him for good measure. As he circled back up the hallway, he heard voices.

"Yes, Master. We'll mobilize all units for patrol," one said.

"Yes, do the job you're supposed to do. Find the bastard," he heard Ezra respond.

Victor dipped into one of the fancy bedrooms, listening through a barely cracked open door.

"Sir, what if he gets one of us first? I have to admit I'm a bit scared. We've never dealt with one of these creatures before. I just…"

The voice stopped. The sounds of cinders crackling and the deeply worrying smell of burnt flesh filled the house.

"You all have more to fear than a fucking hybrid. Let this be an example of what will happen to each of you if you don't catch this bastard," Ezra spoke sternly. "Now get out of my house and get to work."

Victor heard the footsteps scatter, and soon after, the door closed. There was silence. He peered out of the door to see what had happened. There was a pile of smoldering ashes still lying on the floor.

"Come on out. You reek of dog," Ezra said.

Hesitantly, he exited the room.

"Are you going to turn me into a pile of ash too?" Victor asked.

"Not if you don't try to cross me. I have no ill will with you at the moment - other than you sneaking into the house. It's the other one I want," he answered.

"I wasn't sure if I'd be welcomed back in here after what happened. And I couldn't enter through the front door. I didn't know who those people were," Victor said. "Who were they anyways?"

"How much did you hear?"

"Enough to know you have people calling you Master now," Victor remarked. "Must be a big ego boost too. Wish people would call me Master."

"They're a bunch of idiots. That's who they are. But anyways, they're not important," Ezra still ignored the question. "You've obviously located our mutual friend since you reek of him, and it seems he gave you a little love bit there too." He paused for a moment, gesturing a finger in the air towards Victor's once-bitten neck. "Yes, I think you'll still be quite useful. You're going to become my personal messenger boy."

"Like hell!" Victor yelled. "I'm not one of your little minions doing your dirty work. I just want things to go back to the way they were. Before bodies started washing up and you came back into my life."

Ezra jumped into his face. "You owe me, you little piece of shit, after I cleaned up your mess! I saved your fucking dead ass life. What if I gave Tally Atwater a call and told her I knew where her vampiric serial killer was hiding out? That wouldn't go over so well, would it?"

"You're the piece of shit. I never asked you to intervene. You did that all on your own. And had you not, we wouldn't be here right now. Also, you wouldn't call her because then she'd be privy to your little island of secrets. What you are gonna do though, is give me enough food to last the both of us a good while. I know you've got it." Victor stated, but this also gave him an idea for future use for one very ambitious news reporter. "Now get out of my face."

"I'll give you what you need," Ezra said, backing away. "But only because I want to keep the two alive long enough for us to catch the little doggy bastard. Wait here, and I'll go get it for you."

"Oh no. I'm coming with you to make sure you give me the right stuff. I don't trust you any farther than I could throw you. And we both know I could throw you off this island if I wanted to." Victor followed him into the elevator.

"I'd like to see you try…" Ezra smiled, pushing the button to the lab and the elevator took them down.

The doors opened and Victor could see the mess from before had been cleaned up. The broken window was already repaired, and new locks had been added to the stainless-steel coolers.

"You work fast," he noted as they exited. "Extra security, eh."

"Should have already been there," Ezra shook his head, repeating…. "Should have been on there before I decided to let you bring some random prey into my house."

"Again, you interjected on your own," Victor said, continuing to observe his every move, but this time also looking around for anything that might be of use. "You still haven't told me who those people were. Why were they dressed like evil monks? And what was with all the formalities outside?"

"Alright! Alright! You're gonna find out sooner or later. We are part of a group of ancient vampires dating back to the late 1500s, working together to preserve our kind. What you may not be aware of is our kind is on the verge of extinction. You would know this if you weren't so shallow," Ezra explained vaguely. "Our work ensures our race will service."

"Couldn't we just make more vampires? Why the whole hybrid thing?" Victor quizzed.

Without answering, Ezra unlocked and opened one of the coolers, pulling out two bags of synthetic blood. He locked it again and turned to hand them to Victor. He took the two but was puzzled when Ezra walked towards the elevator.

"Excuse me, but I'm gonna need some from that one as well." He pointed towards the cooler containing the werewolf extractions.

"Oh, you want that too? Well, you don't want much, do you? All in due time. You'll take this for now, and we'll see how things work out. I don't expect your little pup will be on the loose for three months. Actually, I don't expect him to be on the loose much longer than a week. So, you see, I'm really wasting the two pints I've already given you." Ezra entered the elevator. "Now come on before the little mutt tries to come in here and find you himself. Can't be too much fun out there hiding behind a bush…unless he's out there pissing on it."

"You knew?" What the fuck, man!" Victor yelped. "Why don't you kill us now?"

"I've already told you I have no intentions of killing you. You're one of us, whether you like it or not. You always did like playing house like one of the prey, but killing you… That would hurt our cause. Him, on the other hand, I could smell him the minute he stepped foot on the property, but… why give up the thrill of the hunt so easily? Where's the fun in that."

"You're sick. You know? Fucking sick!" Victor said, filling Ezra's hand rub the small of his back. He tried to pull away, but it followed.

The elevator door opened back onto the main floor and Ezra ushered him towards the front door. As he opened it, he made one more remark, leaving Victor feeling even more uneasy.

"If it makes you feel better, I don't want to kill him, either. I want to keep him as a pet and train him. You see, it's easier to train a pup to listen to its master when it's young." Ezra flashed his smirky smile and closed the door in Victor's face.

Victor walked away from the front porch, over to the bushes where they'd been hiding out. Charlie was nowhere to be found. *Good luck training this pup, Ezra.* He looked around but didn't see any signs of him. Panic set in for a moment, but he quickly calmed himself down when he caught a whiff of him on the breeze. As he stuffed the blood bags into his pocket, he felt a piece of paper in there. He'd almost forgotten about the map he'd found in the office. To keep the condensation forming on the outside of the still-cold bags of blood from damaging the map, he reorganized the contents of his pockets and headed in the direction of the smell.

A short walk later he found Charlie sitting under a tree in a wooded area. He jumped up to meet him as he approached.

"Man, I couldn't stay there. When I saw those strange people coming back out, I didn't know what was going on," he explained. "One of them was missing and you were still in there. I figured you could handle yourself, and I needed to get out of sight before they came for me and…"

"It's ok. I'm fine. You're fine. He already knew you were there," Victor interrupted his frantic explanation.

"Wait, what do you mean he already knew I was there?" he asked.

"We need to get you another lavender bath. He could smell the both of us. But I think I've found something." He handed him the map. "It's a map of the island and appears to be marked up with X's and lines. Maybe the fences?"

Charlie looked at the map. "Maybe not, but these X's, this is something. They're the power stations on the island. I've seen a few of them. When the time comes, if we cut the island's power, we could hopefully kill this whole operation."

"That's a fantastic idea, though, with the way he is, he's probably got backup generators all over the place." Victor pointed out, adding: "But I have another idea. It might prove to be more fruitful. He threatened to call Miss Atwater and tell her where I was if I didn't do what he wanted me to do, but he'd never really do it, and I called him out on it. But what if we actually did that?"

"Did what?"

"What if we called her and told her about the missing families on the island? We could even send her the video footage you found on the alarm system. If we did it anonymously, she'd never know," Victor explained.

"And someone as ambitious as her would definitely snoop around. It might at least create a distraction until we can come up with another plan," Charlie remarked, moving off toward the house they now permanently referred to as "the castle". "Come on let's get over there now and start working on extracting the files."

"And getting you another bath," Victor joked, taking Charlie's hand in his as they navigated the woods.

# Chapter Sixteen

## The Best Defense...

Tally Atwater sat at her desk when an email from the anonymous tip box came through to her laptop computer. She didn't normally pay these any attention as it was mostly bullshit news watchers trying to get on television. The number of people who claimed to see a vampire in the Kitty Hawk area continued to grow. There were more claims of vampires than there were residents on the island, but this one caught her eye. This particular email not only came with a claim but also with video evidence.

She opened the email and began reading a horrific story about how the inhabitants of an entire island only a few hours south of her had mysteriously vanished, and the sender believed they had evidence of how it happened.

Something like this hadn't occurred since the lost colony of Roanoke in 1590 when a new group of settlers vanished off Roanoke Island without a trace. The only thing found was the word CROATON carved into a post by the settlement's fort. If it were true, this was a reporter's dream of a lifetime - and the big break she'd been waiting for.

She closed up her laptop and b-lined it to her boss' office where she pleaded her case to go down and investigate. She was adamant there would be a connection between Figure Eight Island and the events in Kitty Hawk. She played him the video clip showing the family being ravaged by the intruders in hopes it would help her case.

"Tally, I appreciate your enthusiasm, but how do you not know this is not a doctored video or even some theater group putting on a performance so they can get on TV?" her boss replied cynically. "We don't have the funds to send you down there with a cameraman and van. We need you here in our own backyard. It's not our job to investigate other people's jurisdictions."

"But, sir, if you'd let me go down there, I'm sure I could make it worth your while. Imagine if your news station was the one to break the story of a new 'Lost Colony'. You'd have the funds to do whatever you wanted," Tally pleaded.

"You've got my answer. If it makes you feel better, send the video to analysis. When they come back and tell you it's a fake, you will understand my reasonings. Now let's get out there and report on how local businesses are going to suffer if they close these beaches," he said, all but pushing her out of the office and closing the door behind her. She turned around, facing the closed door behind her. Frustration in every inch of her face.

"You're not taking away my agency!" she snarled militantly, fist balled up in the air.

Tired of being cockblocked by The Man, she took matters into her own hands. She would send the video to analysis alright, just to prove him wrong. And she was also going down to Wilmington. She only needed to find a way to escape the office.

Sitting back at her desk she looked at the history of the island. She decided to gather as much information as possible while awaiting the return of the video analysis. History showed the island comprised approximately four-hundred-seventy-five homes and was primarily inhabited - or previously inhabited - by some of the world's most elite. A guard tower watched over the entrance around the clock, so getting onto the island was going to prove difficult. The more she googled the more far-fetched it seemed everyone could quite-frankly disappear, but the video played heavily in her mind. *If there was limited access to the island, no one would really know if a gang of vampires flew in and devoured them one by one.* She thought, passionately: *"I've got to get on this island."* She closed up shop once more, this time gathering her keys, purse, phone, and whatever bare necessities she felt she would need.

"Philipé, come with me!" she shouted as she headed towards the news station door. "Lisa, cover for me. I've got a big story. I'll keep you posted."

Philipé followed behind her, his camera and boom mic in tow.

"Tally, hold up!" he said, running to catch up. "Where we going?"

"I've got a tip on something and I'm not letting this pompous jerk keep me from breaking this story," she replied. "He won't give me a van. That's fine. I'll take my own car."

"Whoa whoa whoa! Do we have approval for this?" he questioned nervously, watching Tally climb up into the driver's seat of her Pathfinder.

"Philipé, do you want to be a part of history in the making or not? Now get in!" She started the car and rolled down the windows to let out the humid southern heat.

Philipé tossed the mic and camera into the back and jumped into the passenger seat.

"Where we going?" he asked.

"Destination: Wilmington. Ground zero - Figure Eight Island," she snapped back, throwing the SUV into reverse, wheels screeching as she threw it in drive and floored it out of the parking lot.

During the five-hour drive, she explained her theories on what may have occurred. Vampires were taking over the coast of North Carolina. Not only did it explain the mysterious deaths in Kitty Hawk, but the video also actually showed proof of it taking place in Wilmington. She knew analysis would determine the video was genuine.

The one theory she wanted to prove the most was a connection to The Lost Colony. How five hundred years ago, a colony of English settlers had mysteriously vanished. What if an army of vampires had something to do with the disappearances as well? It was far-fetched, she knew, but what if it wasn't? What if she was on to something?

It was dusk when they arrived at the guards' gate to the island. Streetlights had started to illuminate the area, but no one was around. The gate was open. They slowly drove through the area expecting to be stopped from entering, but no one stepped out of the guards' house.

"If that ain't creepy!" Philipé remarked.

"Yeah, what happened to the guards? An island full of elitists would definitely be heavily guarded. At least I'd like to think so," Tally said, looking back in the rearview mirror once more before the guards' house disappeared from view and they cruised over the drawbridge.

Driving onto the island was even creepier than passing the guards' house. It was dark. There were no signs of life. Every over-the-top house they passed sat dead to the world. They passed a white dilapidated sign reading: "Governed by the Figure Eight Homeowners' Association."

"Not anymore," Philipé commented.

"No shit! What the hell happened out here?" Tally cried out in amazement, adding, "It's completely deserted."

They nearly jumped out of their seats when her phone rang. Immediately recognizing the station's number, she sent it to voicemail and flipped it to silent mode. She was on a mission and no representative of the patriarchy was gonna stop her from breaking this to the world.

Victor and Charlie sat outside on the castle's porch discussing old vampire lore, and the differences between the movies, books, and video games. But mostly, how it all applied to them in real life.

"What about sunlight?" Charlie asked. "Didn't think we were allowed to be in the sunlight."

"Being in the sun is a benefit of feeding. The more you feed, the longer you can withstand the sun," Victor explained. "There's no telling really how long the synthetic blood created by Ezra and his minions will last in that respect. We've been on this island for a little over a week and haven't had any issues - though my guess is we will find out when the sun starts to burn us to a crisp."

"I guess it's better than spending the rest of your life in the dark," Charlie quickly tossed in. "This also explains why you left me in the middle of the night. So many things make sense now. The lack of food in the house, seeing you on the dock… you… appearing out of nowhere to scare the shit out of me… But if that's the case, how long does feeding on a person normally last?"

"Prey. We refer to them as prey," Victor answered. "It makes it less personal when you look at it as a food chain with the likes of us at the top. A normal feeding of prey can last anywhere from a few days to a week. And you must drain them completely dry. Failure to do so will create a whole supply of children with you as the baby's daddy. You will have to take care of all of them by yourself. Gives a whole new meaning to when people refer to children as crotch goblins when you think about it.

"Man, that's ridiculous. Note to self, drain

everyone," Charlie laughed. "Though, I kinda like the thought of being a 'Daddy."

"Was always my motto… until I met you," Victor looked up from the stake he was whittling and into Charlie's eyes. "And I bet you do, Daddy."

"But you didn't drain me. That sorry ass bastard of an ancient piece of shit did," he said. "Partially anyways, otherwise, we wouldn't be sitting out here making stakes. Does this shit still work anyways? Seems a little ancient in itself. Can't we find something more creative? Things are so much more advanced these days."

"I'm sure we could, though. We'd want to be sure the same instruments won't be used on us. For instance, I don't want one of those minions turning around and using a nail gun to shoot me in the head, heart, dick, or wherever else they'd try to hit," Victor replied.

"Give me a flame thrower or a rocket launcher any day," Charlie scoffed. "I'd take all them bitches out at the same time."

"That might prove useful at some…" Victor paused, and silence fell over the conversation as headlights suddenly appeared over the hill. Charlie jumped up, running inside to grab the handgun from the kitchen counter. Presumably, it was another of Ezra's cronies doing patrol around the island – but you never knew… They stood on alert watching the white SUV slowly pass the house between the Leyland cypress trees lining the road.

"Who's the hell is that?" Charlie asked. "This is the first sign of civilian traffic we've seen since we've been here."

"I think our best defense has just arrived," Victor said, standing down.

# Chapter Seventeen

## And So... It Begins...

"Have you found them yet?" Ezra yelled over the phone. "Damnit! Get your asses out there and find those motherfuckers! Not only do we have a hybrid on the loose, now we've got two civilians running amok on the island. Someone get that damn guard station back up and running! We can't let anyone else get on this island. Call me when you have them!"

"Fuck! Fuck! Fuck! Fuck!"

Ezra was at his wits' end. This was absurd. How could a bunch of five-hundred-year-old men be so incompetent? If he could, he'd kill them all and go after the trespassers, but that would implicate himself far too much in the grand scheme of things. He needed to be careful should anything happen. After all, the others were there to take the blame.

He went to the elevator and used his ring key to access the secret button taking him down to the containment center. The doors opened, revealing what had once been a young man – but now a dried-up corpse. A wolf corpse, that is. He walked over to the keypad to enter the passcode and the robotic arms retracted. The captives' screams rang in his ears as he hoisted the corpse off the gurney and thrust it into the incinerator in the back of the room. The stench of burning flesh began to slightly overpower the smell of human waste piling up inside the cages. He rarely bothered to clean it out, and maybe if they'd stop shitting themselves every time he walked into the room, it wouldn't be so bad.

"Anyone want to volunteer?" he said, taunting them as they backed into the corners of the cages. "Of course you don't. You're all a bunch of sheep. Like we all were some five hundred years ago when we settled in this godforsaken land. I was one of you once - a settler escaping the rule of the great Virgin Queen. But the gods did not forsake me. No. They made me one of them."

He walked over to the large stainless-steel refrigerators, slopping something onto a tray as he continued his gallant speech:

"They saw something in me. A vision of greatness, I presume. I was one of the few they kept alive out of the hundred and seventeen people left there to start the great New World. And what a great New World did we start! Look at you all! Give yourselves a hand! This is a great way for you all to contribute to the continuation of this world. You… with all your financial advantages - and some of you are the biggest stars Hollywood has ever seen."

He tossed the tray on the floor and slid it under one of the cages.

"Now where has that gotten you? Locked in a cage. That's where it's gotten you. Some of you sought refuge on the island thinking it was a great place to keep your secrets. Your secrets of bestiality. Yeah, you heard me. Out here sleeping with these wolves - making more wolves - like the young man who recently gave his life for the great cause."

"You may ask yourselves, 'Why am I telling you all this?' Because it's not going to matter one way or the other. You're all going to receive the same fate as our young friend here soon. Maybe next time one of you will volunteer instead of me having to…"

"Here, I volunteer! Take me!" said the woman who'd yelled out before. "You've already taken my son. I have nothing else to live for."

He thought for a moment then flashed that

smirkish grin. "Nah, I'll let you suffer down here a little longer."

His phone let out a loud ring echoing throughout the chamber.

"Hello? You've got them? Where? 'Bout time you did something right. I'll be there shortly. Don't hurt them till I get there."

He continued with his captive guest by grabbing the closest one by the collar. This one put up much more of a struggle. Grabbing a metal pole from a table nearby, he knocked it over the head as yet another example of what would happen if anyone defied him. With one swoop he tossed the flaccid chunk of meat onto the gurney and set the machine up to harvest. He didn't even bother adjusting the arms to a proper placement. Wherever they struck would work fine for this one. There were more important things to take care of now. Giving them all a wave, he exited into the elevator and ascended to the main floor.

Victor and Charlie looked on from the trees as the robed figures surrounded the two individuals Victor immediately recognized as Tally Atwater and her cameraman. The two were sitting, hands tied behind them, back-to-back on the sand behind one of the houses. The ocean, not far off in the distance.

"Well, that didn't take long. Figured they'd at least get to roam around for a full day before getting themselves captured," Charlie said. "And don't these people ever wear anything other than robes?"

"We have to help them, I mean the woman irked me to no end, but…" Victor commented thoughtfully, but added: "After all, it's our fault they are here in the first place."

"Oh, we're definitely helping them. It's a matter of finding out how," Charlie commented. "We can't go out there fangs a-blazin' so to speak. They'll suck the life out of them before we could even get there."

"Maybe not. They'd have done it already if they were going to. I wonder why they haven't?" Victor asked. "Something's up… No, literally… Look"

He pointed up in the sky as a dark misty cloud moved in, closer and closer. Except this was no beachy afternoon storm cloud. He knew exactly what - or rather who - it was. Ezra must have special plans for these two if he made them await his arrival. The cloud quickly formed a funnel to the ground as Ezra appeared at its base - triumphantly before them all.

"I can't stand here and do nothing," Victor said.

"Be careful. Stay safe, and… I love you." His mind not registering it was the first time he'd said the words out loud.

He took off running out of the woods towards the group of people, hearing a rumbling roar behind him. Turning back, he saw Charlie was transforming. This was it. This was going to be the fight where they took a stand. There was no going back now.

Victor stopped barely short of the group and shouted, "Let them go, Ezra! They have no part in this!"

"Hey, I know you!" Tally said, turning her head as far as her restraints would allow, to see Victor.

"Oh, but they do. You see, you brought them into this. I simply can't allow them to leave," Ezra replied. "That would be… rather quite careless of me. Unless you want to confess to all the chowing down you did up in Kitty Hawk. Yes, I think a confession is in order. Miss Atwater, wouldn't you like to meet the person behind all those dead bodies you had to report on?"

Tally's body shook left and right as she struggled in her restraints, yelling "Let me go you crazy fuckers!"

"A confession? For what, you ancient fool?" Victor yelled. "You're not letting any of us off this island without a fight and a fight you're going to get. Whatever you're doing on this island, it ends here!"

"Oh, you poor, stupid, pretty boy, this is only the beginning. There are many other places like this around," Ezra said, walking towards Victor, but as he did Charlie landed on all fours between them. "Oh look, you brought your pup along to play. Not today good boy, not today," he teased and turned to the robed men. "Load them up in the cars!"

The four robed men reached down to lift Tally and her cameraman off the ground, but before they had a chance to lay a finger on them, Victor - with his super-powered speed - ran in between, driving a stake into the heart of the smallest one, who fell to the ground, his body twitching violently, shriveling up, and turning to ash as he died. The others stepped back in fear watching their friend die before regrouping and surrounding Victor who opened his mouth - fangs out in the open - letting out a hiss.

Charlie had taken off again, leaving Ezra to stand off in the short distance observing what'd taken place. He flipped his wrist, and the remaining three men went flying in the air, landing roughly fifty feet away on the sand - the impact rendering them unconscious. He came charging towards Victor, but he ducked down and dipped to the left as he went passing by. Turning around to see what was coming next, he noticed Charlie running towards one of the robed figures on the ground, but he came to a sudden halt and let out a whimper. Victor turned in the opposite direction. Ezra's right hand was up as if holding someone by the throat.

"You let him go!" he shouted. "You let him go right now! You said you wouldn't hurt him."

"Ah, but you made the first move, my dear, by interrupting our business," Ezra pointed out. "Putting your precious pup in the line of fire. As much as I'd like to keep him, he's expendable. Might slow me down a little, but I can make another one."

"You piece of shit! I"m gonna…"

But before he could finish his sentence, Tally jumped up, grabbed the boom mic, and knocked Ezra over the head with it - hard. He lost his concentration but still managed to send Charlie flying into a tree. Victor heard a loud whimpering sound coming from where he'd landed, but he was nowhere to be seen. He quickly ran over to Tally and Philipé, helping them up and untying the rest of Philipé's ropes. Ezra sat up on the sand as they ran off towards the woods.

"Get up, you fools!" he yelled.

The robed men rose to their feet but were seemingly still unconscious as they floated a few inches above the ground. Victor turned to see Ezra now controlling them with his hands. This amount of power was something he'd never seen from him before as the three men's lifeless bodies gathered to block their escape. They stopped in their tracks pinned between two horrendous evils, with nowhere to turn.

# Chapter Eighteen

## The End...Or Is It?

Victor surveyed their surroundings. To the left, there was another abandoned house. To the right, a pier leading out to the beach. Behind them, three floating bodies under the control of someone - or something - else. In front of them, nothing but open beaches and the evilest man he'd ever known. He could make a run for it, grabbing Tally and Philipé under his arms, but in all truthfulness, it probably wouldn't work. Ezra would catch them. It was obvious he was far more powerful than he ever let on. As he was coming to terms with the brutal truth that there was no escape and he'd led the other two to their deaths, he heard something that gave him hope.

"Drrroooooopppppppp!!!"

He pulled Tally and Philipé down to the ground as

Charlie leaped in from above - no longer in wolf form and completely naked. In his hands was the flamethrower he'd found the day before. *Damn, these rich people were good for something.* As he was coming in for a landing, Victor took off towards the pier. Tally and Philipé followed suit. The heat from the flames singeing the ends of her hair as they escaped.

When they were in the clear, Victor turned noticing the three floating men were now lying on the ground burning to ashes - Charlie continued to douse them in flames. Ezra had ascended into the sky. Victor wasn't surprised. The coward probably knew four against one would be a challenge for him. And he wouldn't want to take the risk of being burned to death on his precious beach. *Oh, but that time was coming.* The three walked over to Charlie.

"Babe. Babe! You can stop." Victor said. "They're gone."

He dropped the flame thrower and embraced Victor, planting a big wet sloppy kiss on him.

"Ughhh… You reek… and…umm… hey… you're much stronger than me. Remember?" Victor barely managed to get out. "Don't kill me, too."

But a female voice interrupted them… "So… umm…I hate to break up this little love connection, but I'm gonna need you guys to start talking, and now, before I go back to Kitty Hawk and expose you all."

In their reunion, they'd almost forgotten about Tally…

"Yeah, let's take a walk," Victor said, ushering them towards the pier.

"Is he going to put on some clothes?" she asked.

"Probably not," Victor replied explaining the events of the last couple of months, or past one hundred years for that matter. Tally listened intently, taking it all in like the reporter she was.

"And the guy floating in the sky, that's the master vampire?" she quizzed. "And the others were his followers?"

"Correct. And while we're sure he's a master vampire, we're not sure if he's the only one, especially with the comment he made about other locations," Charlie chimed in, swinging his flame thrower around in his hand like a baton.

"There's more than one?" Tally asked. "Where are they? Hidden around here somewhere?"

"We're not sure. This is the main one we're focusing on right now. It's kinda personal, and we could really use some help," Victor said. "That's why we sent you the video footage."

"That was you? You really did bring me into all

this!" she yelled.

"We're sorry. We didn't mean to use you both as a trap. It merely kinda happened," Charlie said, adding swiftly, "So what do you say? Do you wanna help us or not? This is far more adventurous than telling the news in the little town of Kitty Hawk! Come on! What do ya think?"

"We did make a pretty good team back there. Didn't we?" she said.

"Speaking of, how did you get out of those ropes so fast?" Philipé asked.

"Honey, don't ever underestimate the power of a woman and a good nail file," she snapped. "I always keep one in my back pocket."

"So, what happens now?" Philipé asked, looking to Victor and Charlie for some kind of guidance.

The four of them reached the end of the pier, the wind blowing in their hair as they looked out over the ocean. The dark misty cloud, now far off in the distance, could barely be seen heading back towards the compound. As it funneled down to the ground, they all watch - Charlie in the buff with his flame thrower tossed over his shoulder, Tally filing her nails, Philipé awaiting an answer, and Victor twirling a stake in his hand.

"We go to war."

To be continued…

# About The Author

Jason Roach is an American Writing Awards award-winning finalist in LGBT+ Fiction & Thriller Fiction for his book The House on Dead Man's Curve – inspired by his personal paranormal experiences in life. He is also the owner and editor-in-chief of Gold Dust Publishing, a new indie publishing company for LGBTQIA+ and Ally authors. A paranormal enthusiast, he previously spent three years as a core member of the Association of Paranormal Study. He has previously been a paranormal/Sci-fi/writing guest panelist or presenter at GalaxyCon, Jordancon, ConCarolinas, and Congregate 9 & 10. Originally from Statesville, NC, he now resides in Winston-Salem, NC.

# Follow The Author


Facebook:

www.facebook.com/JasonRoachAuthor

Instagram:

@jasonroachauthor

Twitter:

@JRoachAuthor

TikTok:

@jasonroachauthor

Email:

JasonRoachAuthor@gmail.com

# Also Available From J. S. Roach

- The House on Dead Man's Curve

# Contributions

- Reflections

# Special Thanks to Our Patreon Supporters

Nick Crook

Use the link below to support Gold Dust Publishing and get exclusive access to many different features.

patreon.com/GoldDustPublishing

# Also Available from Gold Dust Publishing

- The House on Dead Man's Curve
  By J. S. Roach

- Until Death: An Eric Kent Investigation
  By Rey Nichols

- Reflections – Our charity book featuring over 40 authors contributing. (including J.S. Roach)

- The Purple Menace and the Tobacco Prince
  By Wade Beauchamp

- The Sword's Secret: Ancient Wonders – Book 1
  By Chris Cole

Milton Keynes UK
Ingram Content Group UK Ltd.
UKHW030320090824
446663UK00001B/20